The Force o

ETERNITY

alexiferreira.writer@gmail.com

THE FORCE OF FIVE

CHAPTER 1

"Dream, did you eat the last lollipop again?" Hope asks angrily from downstairs; I turn the cherry-flavoured sucker around in my mouth as I step into my room, and then pull it out, making a popping sound.

"Sorry," I call out, and immediately hear Hope muttering to herself. Looking around, I smile. What can I say? If you snooze, you lose. I lift my hand as I walk towards my bed, and let the shiny pieces of glittery fabric that drapes down from my ceiling float through my fingers. I opened my window earlier, and the breeze coming from outside is gently blowing the fabric, making it sway, the colours reflecting off the walls in a glittery sea of light.

I can hear the birds chirping in the trees that surround the house, the sound making me smile. I sit down on my bed and lean back against the headboard, my legs stretched out before me. Rolling the lollipop in my mouth, I smile as the flavour of cherry engulfs my senses. I bring the hand lying in my lap up to the beautiful purple amethyst stone hanging around my neck, and sigh. The stone always brings me peace and makes me smile.

My sisters and I are five Eternity Fairies, all born to the sovereign queen Fairy, our mother. The five of us are very different in our powers, as each one of us has a different gift we share with others. As one of the Eternity Fairies, my job is to help make people's dreams come true. When someone has a dream and works really hard to acquire that dream but sometimes is finding it difficult to make it come true, that is where I come in and give them a little push in the right direction, or sometimes a big push, depending on the situation.

My sisters, Hope, Love, Reality, Vain, and I all live in the middle of Eternity Fae Forest. The house is big enough that we each have our own room, and when looking at each room, it is evident whose rooms they are. We all have our unique way of decorating our spaces. To me, my room is the nicest. It is like a real dream, with lots of colour all around. As a hobby, I make beautiful dreamcatchers that I sometimes send to people's homes without them knowing where it came from, to help them with bad dreams. My dreamcatchers are specially made for each person, and magically catch all the bad dreams before they can have them. The way I know about people's dreams is with the stone that hangs around my neck. When someone is plagued with nightmares, my stone warms and starts to shine its beautiful purple light. As I touch it, an image of the person having the dreams will appear in my mind. I close my eyes and walk into their dreams to make them more peaceful. I sometimes make a special dreamcatcher and send it to them to help them sleep better at night. They will never know where it came from, but they are so beautiful that everyone ends up hanging them up.

Living deep in the forest helps us find the peace we require from nature, and no one will find us here, but we are still close enough to people to know when they need our help. I love seeing people happy. To be able to contribute to that happiness for me is a blessing. Leaning forward, I pick up the paintbrush I left there earlier. I look at the half-painted wall to my right and smile.

I decided to paint a waterfall, with a stallion poking its head through the cascading water. When the painting is finished, I will be able to go to bed and dream that I am at the waterfall, surrounded by birds and the sound of running water.

"Dream, have you seen Beast?" Love asks from the doorway. Looking over at her, I start to giggle. There is grass all over her hair, and her tights have holes in them, which tells me that

Beast got the better of her once again. Love has an affinity for animals, and Beast, as his name professes, is an animal. He is a cross between a huge dog and a lion. He can be feral when necessary, but is otherwise a real sweetie. He just doesn't know his own strength.

"Did you try to put that collar around his neck again to try to walk him like a pet?" I ask, and she rolls her eyes as she shrugs.

"I will get him to come around. Just you wait and see," she says grumpily as she walks in and comes to sit on my bed. I shake my head in amusement at her persistence. Beast always wins, but she insists on trying to tame him.

"Oh, Love, I do admire your persistence," I say.

"Oh." Love sighs as she gets up from the bed and comes to stand next to me. "It's looking great. I wish I could paint like you." She moves closer to look at the outline of the horse, her hand lifting to touch what looks like glittering water.

"You haven't seen nothing yet. I am using paint that lights up at night." Love looks over at me, shaking her head in awe.

"You are so talented." She steps closer and hugs me close, kissing my cheek. Love has always been the hugging, kissing type. As the love Fairy, she helps those who think love is lost to them, showing them the way. Love has the voice of an angel; she can sing like no one I have heard before. “Well, I better go look for Beast before he destroys something of Vain’s.” We both giggle at that, as Beast likes to pick up Vain’s things. We usually find the things hidden in his bed, all wet from his dribble.

“I’ll come with you.” I don’t want to miss this if he did pick up one of Vain’s things. I throw my paintbrush down and hurry after Love. We head down the corridor to Vain’s room. Getting there, we see her lying on her bed, reading. As we both come to a standstill at her door, she looks up towards us.

“What?” she asks with a raised brow.

“Have you seen Beast?” Love asks as she looks around, not that she has to. With the size of Beast, you can see him immediately wherever he is.

Vain immediately sits up on her bed and points at Love. “He better not have taken anything else of mine,” she states as she starts to look around her room. Vain, as per her name, has self-confidence like no one else I know; she believes that she can do anything she puts her mind to, and she really does conquer whatever project she takes on. Out of the five of us, she is also the most feminine. She loves her makeup, clothes, and nail polish.

Vain plays the guitar like no one ever has before. She can string a tune in simply minutes. Vain has the gift of helping those who have no self-confidence. She builds them up and helps them succeed to become the best version of themselves.

"He hasn't had time to get anything. We went outside, and the minute I placed the collar around his neck, he was off. I tried to hold on to the leash, but you know how he is. The next thing I know, I was on the ground and he was gone."

"Maybe he hasn't come back home," I say as I walk towards Vain's window and look out. I never get tired of looking out and seeing the beauty that is our surroundings. The trees that surround us hide our existence, but they also bring us the energy we need to flourish. As part of the Eternity Fae, we are guardians of alternative beings. To help us, we have the Gargoyles, who protect the cities from unwanted attacks.

We have been at peace for centuries thanks to my mother, the Fairy queen, and my father, the Gargoyle king. Humans don't know we exist, but that is for their protection. I see a movement below coming out of the trees, and smile. Instead of Beast, I see Drez approaching. He is one of our guards and a dream to look at. I don't tell anyone about my fascination with Drez, but I'm sure my sisters suspect.

"Can you see him?" Love asks from across the room.

"No, sorry," I say, turning as I see Drez enter the house.

"I don't know why you are worrying, Love; you know that sooner or later, he will be back," Vain says as she gets up from her bed.

"I know, but he's still a puppy, and I worry about him all alone out there."

"Seriously, the animal is bigger than you. If anything, everything else will run away from him. He will be fine." I can see Love's worry, and I know she won't rest until she finds Beast.

"Okay, let's go see where else he could be," I say, placing my arm through hers and pulling her behind me. I hear Vain closing her bedroom door and quickly following us. Her precaution of making sure that Beast doesn't once again take something from her room makes me smile.

The three of us make our way downstairs, as Love would have looked in Hope's room already, as it's next to hers, and Reality's is next to mine, which she would have seen before getting to me.

"What are the three of you up to?" Reality asks as she approaches from the back of the house, her long light-brown hair bouncing around her shoulder from her ponytail as she walks. Her light-blue eyes look from Love to me and then to Vain.

"Love has lost Beast again; we are going to go look for him," Vain says with a shrug.

"Well, I hate to cut this search party short, but Beast is in the kitchen, eating the meatballs I made for dinner."

"Uuu yum, we haven't had your meatballs in a while," I say as I let go of Love's arm and hurry towards the kitchen. Reality has a magic touch when it comes to cooking. Her food is always to die for no matter what she makes. She doesn't cook enough, though, as we are always busy with our other assignments, but she tries to cook at least once a week to treat everyone. I hear the others following me as I enter the kitchen to find Hope already dishing food onto a plate for herself.

One thing about us is that we can eat as much as we want without having to worry about putting on weight like the humans do. I love eating, and if anyone else in the house hears about Reality's cooking, they will all be down here in a flash. I hope Drez doesn't come down. I look down at my dungarees and groan at the splatters of paint on them.

It doesn't really matter, anyway. He won't look at me when Vain is around. Vain is so pretty that I vanish in comparison. I usually have my long, wavy black hair in plaits, unlike Vain, whose silky light-brown hair is bouncy and perfect around her shoulders. My normal attire is dungarees because they are practical for painting and running outside and climbing trees to hide from my sisters. Vain wears the sexiest dresses that show off her beautiful body.

"If you're not going to dish for yourself, then get out of the way," Vain says, bringing me back to what I'm doing. I also do that a lot—dream. My sisters are always teasing me about it, but my mind seems to wander a lot. I love to dream about things I want to do or places I want to see but can't because of being hidden away in Eternity Fae.

Filling my plate with spaghetti and then the delicious-smelling meatballs, I make my way to the table where Hope is already sitting. I see Love has sat down in front of Beast and is patting his head, murmuring to him. His eyes are closed in pleasure as her fingers stroke his big head.

I sit down opposite Hope to see her frowning at me. "What?" I ask as I take a mouthful of food. Mmm, divine.

"When are you going to stop eating all the lollipops? There is nothing sweet in the house now." Hope has a terrible sweet tooth. She usually doesn't eat many sweets and is more into chocolates, but for her to be after the lollipops, it means she has finished off all the chocolate.

"Look who's talking. You always eat all the chocolate in the house. Why don't you eat those and leave the lollipops alone?" I ask, taking another mouthful of food. Reality comes to sit next to me, a plate in front of her too.

"That's what I just said to you. There aren't any."

"Well, I'm sure our groceries will be arriving soon; I asked for some of those great biscuits I like, and they haven't arrived yet either," Love says as she comes to join us.

"That's strange. We have never run out of stuff; we usually get our groceries twice a week. Do you think they missed a day?" Reality asks as she looks around at us with a frown.

"They have never missed before. If they did now, it must have been for a good reason," Vain says before taking some of the food into her mouth and closing her eyes in pleasure. "This is really great, Rea."

"Thanks. I tried something new," Reality says, and then a surprised look crosses her face. "Now that I think about it, some of my spices were also gone. I think there is definitely something going on, guys."

"Well, what is that wonderful smell that I'm smelling all the way from the top?" I look towards the kitchen door and smile. Brog is standing there, smiling at all of us. Brog has been with us ever since we were babies. He is the captain of the guard here and one of my father's best friends. My parents put their faith in him to keep their daughters safe. He has become that father figure we all miss when ours is away, which is most of the time. Brog is a Werewolf, and as such, he is faster, stronger, and meaner than some evil lurking in the real world. Looking at him, no one would say what he is. With his longish brown hair and muscular body, he looks like any human, but it's when he changes that the changes become very real.

Mother and Father moved us to Eternity Fae Forest when we were just babies to keep us safe while they stayed among the humans. They help protect the humans from all the evil out in the world that they don't even know exists.

"I made meatballs," Reality answers with a smile, which has Brog rubbing his hands exaggeratedly as he walks towards the stove.

"Brog, we were wondering," Vain says.

"Oh boy, that is never good when the five of you get together and wonder," he teases as he fills his plate.

"We have noticed that there are a lot of things missing. Haven't the groceries been delivered yet?" Brog makes his way towards the table. I see by the way he tenses at the question, he doesn't want us to know, but as Fae, we always know when someone is lying to us.

"Actually, no, it hasn't." We look around at each other and then again at him. There has never been a time that the delivery has missed, or at least, not that we know about.

"Has that happened before?" I ask.

"No, it hasn't," he says, placing his fork next to his plate. He places his elbows on the table as he looks around at all of us. "The groceries haven't been delivered twice now when they should. We have been at the meeting point, but no one has appeared." He rubs his face with his hand, indicating that he's stressed but hasn't wanted to show us.

"We have tried to contact them, but there has been no reply." My stomach knots in fear. Has something happened to our parents? They would never have gone two weeks without contacting Brog to find out how we were doing. "I didn't want to worry you, as I'm sure this is nothing, but I have decided that tomorrow, I am going into the city to see what is going on."

"No, Brog," Love says as she stands up. At her agitation, Beast stands and makes his way towards her. He now stands behind her, his eyes watchful as he senses her worry. "You can't go and leave us here alone. What if something happens to you?"

"He will be fine. Don't worry, Love, I'm sure everyone is fine. This must be some kind of miscommunication," Hope says. Hope, as her name suggests, has a perchance for only assuming the best of situations. She usually brings hope to those who have lost all hope in their life. She is also gifted with an amazing green finger. When we can't find Hope, we know she is out in the forest among nature. She can make anything grow, even when it looks like it's nearly dead.

"No, let's think about this," Reality says. "We have been receiving our groceries every week without fail for years and years, and now for two weeks, it has stopped. Mom and Dad faithfully contact Brog every week to know about us and talk to us, but as far as I know, they haven't contacted any of us in a while. Am I wrong?" She looks at Brog.

Brog shakes his head. "I'm sure it's nothing. I have prepared the men for the days I will be away, and I promise that as soon as I get out there and know something, I will contact you and let you know."

My heart is racing. We have never been in a situation like this before. What could possibly be happening out there in the world?

CHAPTER 2

It has been three days since Brog left, and he still hasn't contacted us. We are all worried about what could be happening, but we have been so busy that we haven't had much time to sit down and think about it. I feel the amethyst around my neck vibrate, a gentle colour radiating. These last few days have increased where nightmares are concerned. I could ignore the pleas, but that's just not like me.

Holding the stone in my hand, I close my eyes. Instantly, a flash of what looks like fire appears in my mind. It looks like this person is dreaming about a fire. Prodding gently into their conscious, I see a teenage boy being held down by what looks like two black shadows. The boy is clearly the one dreaming, but I wonder where he got the idea of these dark shadows from.

Lifting my hands, I murmur the sounds associated to light. Brightening his dream, I then imagine a great big cloud moving in from above where these shadows are still holding down the teenager, and let the cloud open up and the rain fall down, washing away the flames. The shadows I see take a while to let him go, but as the dream brightens and the scenery starts to change, the shadows get sucked into the ground and disappear. When I am sure that he is once again sleeping in peace, I open my eyes to find Hope leaning against the door of my room.

"Another nightmare?" she asks, nodding towards my stone.

"Yeah, there have been so many lately," I say as I lean back against my headboard, feeling the calmness of the colours around me.

"You know what I am finding?" Hope asks. "There have been more Fae lately who have needed my help than humans."

That is interesting, as usually, Fae are not beings drawn to losing hope. All Fae are different in one way or another. Hope is ingrained in us from the day we are born.

"That's not right, is it?" I ask.

"No, it's not," she says as she walks into my room. Hope is the firstborn and therefore the oldest of the five of us. Soon, her Fairy wings will make an appearance, and then she will get her full powers. We fairies don't age like humans; we are considered teenagers still, and meanwhile, in human years, Hope would be seventy-five years old.

"Do you think it has anything to do with what is happening?"

"I d—"

"Brog is back. I saw him from my window," Reality says as she runs past the door of my room. Hope and I look at each other and then run out of the room and after Reality. We are nearly at the bottom of the stairs when the front door opens and Drez and Trek are helping Brog inside, one on each side of him.

"Brog, you're hurt," Reality states worriedly.

"I'm okay. Nothing a little rest won't cure," he mutters, but he is pale and his massive strength has left him because of his wound.

"Take him to his room. I will take a look and see what I can do," Hope says, which has the other two men leading Brog down the corridor to his room. When he is finally lying on his bed, Hope leans over him to pull his bloodied shirt aside, and then she gasps.

"What did this to you?" she asks. I take a step forward, as I can't see from where I'm standing, and then gasp. There are what look like claw wounds on Brog's chest and side. It looks like some big beast wounded him.

"I don't know. It was like fighting shadows." He closes his eyes in exhaustion.

"It's looking enflamed," Hope says as she probes around the deep wounds. "Dream, go get fresh water; Reality, bring clean clothes." She looks around at Trek and Drez, who are standing to the side, awaiting instructions. "Please undress him. When you are done, call me back in," I hear her instructing the men as I hurry out of the room.

I rush to the kitchen, finding Selina washing a bowl of fruit in the sink. We could say that Selina takes care of us in our mother's stead. She's an Elf with beautiful blonde hair that reaches the base of her back. Selina is a gentle soul, but I know that if push comes to shove, she can be as protective as any other Fae, if not more. "What's the hurry, Dream? Whatever it is won't run away," she says with a calm smile.

"Brog has been hurt. Hope needs water to clean the wounds."

Selina tenses, and I can see the worry on her features. She quickly leans down and pulls out a big glass bowl and starts to fill it with water.

"Go to my room. There is a wick basket under the bed. Bring it to Brog's room. Go. I will take the water."

I turn and hurry to Selina's room. Entering, I see her semi-precious stones all around her room. Selina is the one who forged our stones when we were babies, as she has an affinity with them. I lean down and see the basket Selina was talking about. Pulling it out, I pick it up gently and hurry down the corridor towards Brog's room.

Entering, I see that Brog has been placed under the covers. His chest is bare for all to see the gruesome wounds there. Hope is leaning over him, cleaning away the blood and dirt that might have accumulated in the wound while he made his way back to us. Selina is sitting on the other side of Brog, examining the wounds as Hope cleans them.

"Here you go." I place the basket on the bedside table next to Selina and step back, bumping into someone. Looking over my shoulder, I gasp. "Oh, um, sorry." I quickly move to the other side of the bed. I hadn't seen Drez right behind me. I can feel my cheeks flaming with colour, as he didn't say anything, just flashed me one of his eye-dazzling smiles. Drez is also a decedent from Elves. His features are perfect, with beautiful blue eyes and long blond hair.

I feel an elbow to my side. I turn to look at Love as she leans towards me to whisper in my ear. "Stop drooling." I tense. Oh, she definitely knows that I have a crush on Drez. I glare at her and then look towards the bed where I see Selina opening her basket to reveal various small vials. Each one of them contains different substances of different colours. I make sure to keep my eyes away from Drez. I would die from embarrassment if he knew I fancied him.

"I'm fine. You don't need to worry," Brog says as he opens his dazed eyes. "I will start to mend in no time."

"When did this happen?" Selina asks in her calm voice.

"Yesterday," he murmurs.

"This looks like some kind of dark magic. Brog should have been healing already if this happened to him yesterday; meanwhile, the wounds are still raw and starting to look infected," Selina states as she pokes gently around the wounds.

"What do you think did this?" Trek asks. Trek is one of our guards and a Werewolf like Brog, but that is where the resemblance ends, as Trek is big, and when I say big, I mean big. He is nearly double of Brog, and Brog is big. Trek's arms are thick with muscle, nearly the breadth of both my legs together. From what I have heard, he is an exceptional tracker.

"I'm not sure I haven't seen this before; it looks like the claw scratches of a feral animal, but you see the jagged edges on the wounds? There is no animal I know that has claws like that," Selina says, pointing at a particular wound. "I'm going to place a salve into his wounds to clean them out of any infection. Hope, I need you to work on his wounds to pull out the poison and restore the good."

Hope looks at her in surprise. "How am I going to do that?" she asks with a frown.

"The same way to bring plants to life when they are nearly dying. He is just like one of your plants, Hope. You can expel the bad and fill it with good." I see that Hope is unsure of what Selina just said, but she nods.

"From you, Dream, I need you to go into Brog's subconscious and have him dream of healing." I frown. I can't go into someone's subconscious if the stone doesn't call me to them and they're not having a nightmare.

"I can't do that, Selina," I say, embarrassed. I wish I could help, but my gift doesn't work like that.

"Yes, you can, sweetie, the same way you go in to dispel the nightmares and create a dream. Just close your eyes and see yourself inside Brog's conscious."

"I will try, but I've never done that before. My amethyst guides me," I confess.

"No, sweetie, your amethyst is simply a tool that helps you. It's not your gift."

I close my eyes and concentrate on Brog. I really hope she's right. I would like nothing more than to be able to help Brog. I find myself in complete darkness, and there is a foul smell. I feel a heavy darkness pulling me down. Am I in Brog's mind? I lift my hands and start to murmur the sound associated with light. I see my hands lighting up, but the darkness is so dense that I have to keep murmuring until the light starts to widen, brightening up my view of my surroundings.

At first, I don't see anything, and then as the light starts to push back the darkness, I see what looks like a forest appear. I must be in Brog's mind. It seems like there is something in the darkness looking at me, but I can't see it. I bring my hands to my chest and then thrust them forward to throw light further away. That's when I see what looks like dark shadows quickly disintegrating into the light. Strange. Why do I keep seeing these shadows in the dreams now?

When I am sure that Brog's mind is filled with light and good thoughts, I think of a beautiful bright-green light filling his mind with health and life. I imagine the light traveling through his body to his wounds, healing them, bringing them to life. I don't know how long I stay in Brog's mind, bringing him peace and happy dreams, but when I become aware again of everyone around me, I see that Selina is sprinkling a shimmery powder over what looks like healthier-looking wounds.

"It's your turn now, Love," Selina says, which has me believing that when I was in Brog's mind, Hope must have been working on his wounds.

"Mine?" Love asks, surprised. "What do you want me to do?"

"Brog now needs to feel loved and secure to heal. Everyone knows that people feel better when they are happy and feel cared for and secure. What you do to those people who feel like they don't have any love in their life I want you now to do with Brog." I can see Love's uncertainty, but she moves toward the bed. Hope gets up and moves away so that Love can take her place.

"We should all leave now and let Brog rest. Love will stay with him, and when she is done, Reality will come sit with him until he wakes up. Reality, after all the healing, he isn't going to feel himself. I need you to bring him to reality."

Reality smiles in response and moves towards the chair that Brog has in his room. I notice that Trek and Drez aren't in the room any longer, which means they must have left when I was in Brog's mind.

I turn and follow Hope out of the room, Selina right behind me. "Where is Vain?" I ask, only now realizing that I didn't see her.

"She came in earlier, but I sent her away. Brog will need her once Reality is done with him. She will need to work with him to make sure there are no aftereffects from the attack.

"How did you know we could all do what you asked us to do?" Hope asks as we walk into the kitchen.

"You girls can do much more than you think you can," Selina says as she strokes Hope's face. "This is just the tip of the iceberg. With time, you will grow into all your powers, but if something is attacking us, we will need to find out what it is and be ready to fight it."

"What do you think it is, Selina?" I ask, worried that we might not be strong enough to defend ourselves.

"I'm not sure yet, but Brog's wounds were infected and getting worse by the minute. He would surely have died if we hadn't helped him. The wounds reeked of evil; whatever attacked him is not good." I can feel my stomach tightening in fear.

"Do you think our parents are okay?" I ask.

"Of course our parents are okay, silly," Hope says as she bumps her shoulder against mine.

"Well, the only thing we can do now is wait for Brog to wake up so he can tell us what he found out. After that, we can see where to go from there."

I know there has always been evil out there, but living in Eternity Fae Forest, we have always been protected from that evil. Now for that evil to have penetrated our oasis of peace, it means there must be something very powerful out there that managed to break my mother's magic that kept our little piece of heaven secret, and to be able to outwit all the Gargoyles my father has guarding the entrances to the forest.

"Come, you girls must be tired. I will make you something calming to drink, and then you should go and have some rest. Tomorrow, when Brog awakens, we will know what happened to him."

I walk towards the table. Taking a seat, I lean back and close my eyes. To be honest, I am a little tired, but I have a feeling that this is just the beginning and that I am going to need all the rest I can get, because this storm of evil is just beginning.

CHAPTER 3

It has taken Brog longer to recuperate than usual, but he is now sitting up in bed and finally ready to tell us what happened to him. His men have been walking in and out of the room the whole morning, as he wanted to make sure that they were prepared for whatever is coming before he talked to us.

"You are making me nervous, all standing around me like that," he quips, which immediately has the five of us finding a spot on his bed and sitting down. "That's better." He smiles. "Now, first, I want to thank all of you for what you did. Selina told me how fantastic you were."

"We were pretty cool, weren't we?" Reality says with a proud smile.

"Yes, you definitely were, and Selina says that if it weren't for you, I wouldn't be here."

"I think Selina's potions also had a lot to do with it," I say, which has Brog turning his head to look at me and nodding.

"Yes, she is talented with her potions," he confirms. "But let's talk about what I saw and what I think we might be facing." We have been waiting for this, but now that it's here, I think we are all scared of what he is about to say.

"I went all the way to the edge of the forest, but I couldn't get out. It's like your mother's spell has been reversed, and instead of keeping others out, it is keeping us in." We all look at each other. What could this possibly mean? "I think it's time I tell you something." I feel my heart racing, as his words sound ominous. "Your parents wanted to tell you this when you all came of age, but now that this has happened, it is time you know the truth."

"Just say it already. You are killing us with suspense," Vain says.

"As Selina hinted to you, your powers are more than you or anyone knows, but what your parents and a few know is that they are vast." He lifts his hand to rub his face, as if trying to think of the best words to tell us whatever he is trying to say. "The thing that you girls don't know is that because your father is a Gargoyle, and a powerful one at that, your powers can work for good and bad." We all gasp, looking around at each other.

"What does that mean? We have always only worked for good. Does it mean that we are going to become evil?" Love asks, her hand over her chest; I see that Beast has come to sit at her feet and is now placing his big head on her lap, which nearly covers her whole body. She leans down and rubs her face against his silky fur.

"No, it means that you can if you want to, and hopefully you don't choose to use your dark powers when you do find them, but continue to only use good, but I needed to tell you because what is coming we might all need to use our full powers to ward off."

"Do you know what is coming?" Hope asks as she sits forward to also stroke her fingers through Beast's fur.

"No, but I know it's not good. When I was in the forest, I felt like I had eyes on me. At first, I thought it was the Pixies, but then I started to feel uncomfortable." Brog shifts his weight on the bed, moving higher against the headboard. His chest is bare, which allows us to see that the wounds are healing rapidly and will soon disappear. His strength is returning, and he will shortly be at his post again.

"When did you feel the eyes on you? Was it on the way out?" I ask, curious to know if whatever is out there knows where we are.

"No, I reached the border between the forest and the outside world. It was while I was attempting to find a way out that I started to feel the eyes on me. Anyway, after a day of trying everything, I decided to come back. That is when I started to see the shadows following me."

"The shadows were real?" I ask. I have been seeing shadows in dreams and found it strange, but I never thought they might be real.

"Yes, or as real as can be," Brog says as he looks at me. "The shadows are the ones that attacked me, and as you can see, they did good work of it."

"But how can shadows do that?" Vain asks as she looks down at Brog's healing wounds.

"I don't know, but what I can tell you is that my strength or fighting skills didn't work with these shadows, as they are just that—shadows. My fists went right through them, but when they attacked me, I was injured, so I don't know how it's possible, and I don't know how we can beat a shadow if we can't strike it."

"What about with light?" I say.

"What do you mean?" Brog asks with a raised brow.

"When I went into your mind, everything was dark. I started by lighting up your mind, and that is when I noticed that there were shadows in the darkness, but the more light I projected into your subconscious, the more the shadows retreated."

"Could be, Dream, but how are we going to project light in real life?" Love asks with a frown.

"If they only like darkness, then they should only be attacking at night. Was it dark when they attacked you, Brog?" Reality asks as she stands and walks to the window, looking outside.

"It wasn't night yet, but it was getting dark." I can see the consideration in Brog's features as he scratches his whiskered jaw.

"Maybe we can try to get to the edge of the forest during the day. If we don't find the way out, maybe building a fire will keep the shadows away," Hope says as she looks around at all of us. "Do you think we can somehow project this light? Maybe with these gifts Brog talks about, one of us could do it?"

I know that we all did something we had never done before when treating Brog, but going from there to actually projecting light in real time is something beyond any powers we have. "I don't know, Hope. I wouldn't even know where to begin," Vain says as she stretches her hands before herself.

"Dream, you already do it when you're in someone's dreams. I think that if any of us can do it, it should be you," Reality says as she turns away from the window and looks at me.

"Me?" How can they think I can do something like that? It's one thing doing it in someone's mind. How would I do it without having a dream to fix?

"Reality has a point; you have done it many times. I am sure that it can't be very different from projecting light in a dream," Love says as she looks over her shoulder at me.

"Are you serious? It's all in my mind when I work on someone's dream, but what you are talking about, I actually have to produce light."

"You can try," Hope says with a smile.

"Oh, you guys are barking up the wrong tree," I mutter as I try to think how I could possibly project light into reality. "But I will try."

"Oh, yay," Love says as she leans over Brog's covered legs and hugs me close.

"Don't get too excited before I actually get this right," I mumble.

"It's good that you will try, but the fact still remains that we don't know what these shadows are or why they are in Eternity Fae Forest. I worry that these shadows will try to attack one of you," Brog says.

"Do you think that is what they want?" Love asks with concern in her voice.

"There is something else I need to tell you."

I groan. How many secrets are there?

"I know. I'm sorry that it's me telling you this. I know your parents wanted to be the ones to tell you, but in light of what is happening, I think it's important you all know the truth." Brog lifts his hand and starts to pat the bed next to him as he looks at Reality. When she finally takes a seat, he pats her hand before looking at us again. "You know that your parents had a hard time when they first met, but the problems weren't just because of one being a Fairy and the other being a Gargoyle, because as soon as your mother gave herself to your dad, her magic enhanced his, which let him be the most powerful Gargoyle in existence."

"We all know that. It's so romantic," Love says with a cheeky smile.

"Yes, it is, but it's not that," Brog says. "If anything happens to your parents, you girls need to be strong enough to combat any contestant who wants to be the next sovereign."

"What?" Vein asks as she stands. "Brog, only the strongest of the strong challenge for the sovereign." She points around the room. "Do we look like we can win any challenge one of the others put forward?"

"Maybe not at the moment, but you all have your mother's and your father's strength in you, and no one else in this kingdom has ever been able to beat them."

"But, Brog, we aren't our parents," Reality says with a shrug.

"No, you are more powerful."

"How would you know that?" Love asks as she continues to stroke Beast's head.

"The oracle told your parents when they got together that they would have five daughters and that their daughters would be gifted with great powers, but that those powers attracted envy and betrayal. That is why they have you growing up here in the Eternity Fae Forest, protected from all evil."

"Well, it looks like evil found us," Vain mutters. "So basically you are telling us that we need to figure out what our powers are and do it quickly because our future seems to have caught up to us." She shakes her head in anger. Rising, she makes her way to the door and then leaves.

"I'm sorry, but your parents thought it better that you only be told when you got your wings, but it seems that the time has come for you to know the truth."

"Well, I'm sure we don't need to worry. We will figure a way to breach the spell that is stopping us from leaving, and then we will find out what is going on," Hope says.

"We have the best men here to protect you. They will die before they let anything happen to any of you. This evil that has breached our borders will be conquered, and we will rise above them."

I stand. I know that this isn't Brog's fault, but I really don't want to hear any more about this enemy. I think that the time has come to try to become the best I can be with whatever gifts I have, and for that, I am going to need to practice. The thing is, what am I practicing? Because I don't even know where to start.

"I'm going now. Thank you for telling us, Brog," I say as I also turn and make my way outside. I have had enough of being inside the whole day. If what they say is true, then the shadows only attack at night. Looking up at the sky, I sigh. It is early afternoon, and the sun is still high up in the sky. I need to think, and the best place for me to do that is by the pond.

I make my way through the forest towards the pond. I hear the animals scattering away as I walk, the fragrance of the forest surrounding me. I will talk to Minna for a while. She always helps me see perspective. Minna has been my friend since I was a child. I met her one day while swimming in the pond, and ever since, we have been friends. Minna is an Elven. Her family and her look after the pond and its surroundings. It is beautiful here, with flowers growing all around the pond. Animals always come to drink from it at one time or another.

“Minna,” I call as I sit on my favourite rock and slip my feet into the water. I start to twirl my feet around in the water, knowing that the disturbance will get someone’s attention, and they will soon come to investigate.

“Okay, okay, you have my attention. You can stop now,” Minna says as she comes out of the water a few feet ahead of where I am sitting, her long brown hair floating on the water behind her.

“About time, too. I was nearly falling asleep waiting for you,” I tease, which has Minna splashing me with water. “Hey.” I laugh.

“Sorry, Dream, we’ve just been a little wary around here,” Minna says as she looks around before she approaches the shore, and then pulls herself up onto the rock beside me.

“Why, what’s wrong?”

“There is something not quite right, Dream. The animals are jittery when they come to drink, and I can feel the earth is unsettled. There is something unsettling the life here at Eternity Fae.”

This must mean that whatever evil is out there is closer than we thought. When Brog was attacked near the border to Eternity Fae, I automatically assumed it was still far from home, but it seems that it's not.

"What's wrong? I can tell by your face that you know something," Minna says as she turns towards me fully.

I don't want to create fear, but if there is evil out there, then I must warn Minna so that her and her family can be vigilant. "What I am going to tell you is not certain yet, but I want you all to be careful." I tell Minna what we suspect about the shadows and that we have been cut off from the outside world. What I don't tell her is our role in all of this. I still don't understand it myself, so I won't be sharing something that might not yet be certain.

"Oh, that's why the Hobgoblins have been uneasy," Minna says, inclining her head towards the forest. "Braun was here yesterday, and you know him—he's not much for words, but he was grumbling about something messing with his oak."

Hobgoblins live in trees. Their preference is oak trees. They are very protective of their homes. Usually calm, peaceful beings, they can become confrontational and will fight whoever threatens them or their home.

Braun lives in a beautiful big oak just down the path. On the way back home, I will stop by and try to find out what has him upset.

"You have a guard?"

At Minna's question, I tense, looking around at what she means, but I don't see anything. "What do you mean?"

"Don't tell me you don't know?" Minna says with a raised brow.

"Know what?" I look around again with a frown.

"One of your men has followed you and is standing guard just behind that big tree before the start to the pond." I turn around on my perch and am just in time to see what looks like a hand moving behind the tree.

"Who is there?" I have never been followed before. Why would one of our men decide to follow me? All thought leaves me when I see Drez stepping away from behind the tree. I jump up in surprise and lose my balance. "Ahhh," I scream, my arms flailing to try to keep me upright, but I am already out of balance. I start falling back. I feel Minna's hand try to grab on to me, but it's too late, and I hit the water back first. I feel myself sinking, and for a minute, I wish I could stay under this water. The embarrassment of now facing Drez has me wanting to bury my head in one of the dunes in the pond. Straightening my body, I kick my legs to take me up to the surface, feeling a hand around my arm as I break through the water.

The first thing I see is Minna's smiling face sitting on the rock where we were together. My head snaps to my side, and I see Drez treading water beside me. The hand holding my upper arm is his, a worried look in his eyes as he watches me. "Are you okay?" he asks, embarrassing me even more as I see his wet blond hair covering one eye.

Why am I such a klutz when he's around? "Umm, fine, you just surprised me." I can feel my heart racing at his touch and my stomach knotting. His deep-blue eyes look at me as if he can see right into my soul.

"Are you going to stay in there the whole day? I can come in and join you, but you must be a little uncomfortable with all those clothes," Minna teases from where she's sitting. I look over and glare at her, knowing she is enjoying this. Drez lets go of my arm and then pulls himself out of the pond, his clothes soaking wet. The loose off-white tunic that he usually wears is plastered to his body, his breeches and dark-brown boots just as wet. As an Eldrin from the high Elves, Drez was born a warrior, his fluid movements catching the eye and holding it like a tree blowing in the breeze.

"Dream?" Minna calls with a laugh. "Are you enjoying your swim?"

"Oh, keep quiet," I mutter as I place my hands on the edge to pull myself out, but before I can, strong arms are pulling me out in one fluid movement and helping me stand.

"Umm, thank you," I whisper, feeling awkward, as I can just imagine how I am looking standing here before him with my dungarees hanging down my body with the weight of the water, and my dark brown hair plastered to my head.

Drez nods and then looks up at the sky. "I think we should be getting back; it's going to start getting dark soon."

I ignore his comment, instead concentrating on what I really want to know. "Why were you following me?"

"I was assigned to keep you safe."

I feel my disappointment rise. He wasn't following me because he wanted to make sure I was fine. He was following me because he was told to. My disappointment weighs heavy on me. I say goodbye to Minna, promising to come see her soon, and then I set out towards home, not once looking back to see if Drez is following me.

I am so upset that only when I reach home do I remember that I was going to go talk to Braun. I will have to go see him tomorrow.

CHAPTER 4

"Come on, you're not trying hard enough." I open my eyes and glare at Vain.

"Really, I haven't seen you doing anything," I argue. Since coming home, the girls ambushed me, insisting we should start practicing. We have been at it for hours, and I still haven't been able to do anything.

"Well, if you girls continue fighting each other, you will not be able to do what you want to." I turn, hearing Selina. She is standing at the door with a kind smile like she usually does. "The five of you are stronger together than apart. You need to support each other, build what you have, and make it invincible. If the five of you are united, nothing will ever be able to break you or beat you."

Selina steps into the room. We have all decided to practice in the sitting room, as it gives us enough space to try our hand at whatever we are trying to accomplish. In my case, it's light, but I'm starting to believe that I'm not the one to wield that power.

"Maybe I can help. Let me see what you are doing," Selina says, looking at Love. Love lifts her arms and starts to twist her hands around in a spiral formation, but nothing happens. After a couple minutes, she drops her arms, pouting. "What are you trying to do?" Selina raises a brow.

"Oh, it's a new dance she's trying to master," Reality teases, which has all of us laughing except for Selina, who shakes her head, and Love, who raises her hands to her hips in annoyance.

"Well, you would know. Standing with your feet spread like that, you look like a gawking goblin." Reality looks down at her feet in surprise and then back up at Love before breaking out in gales of laughter.

"Okay, let's do this instead," Selina says as she walks towards one of the couches and sits down. "How about you tell me what you are thinking of wielding and how you propose to do it, and from there, maybe we can help each other by suggesting better options or trying it yourselves. Who knows, you might find that one can't do it but another one can."

"Well, I am trying to manifest light, but everything I have tried hasn't worked," I say as I approach Selina. I see her wise eyes looking at me as I stand before her.

"How do you manifest light when you're in a dream?"

I bring my index finger up to my lips as I think of the best way to explain. "I start by murmuring the mantra for light. I lift my hands and visualize the light radiating from them, shining wherever I want it to go."

"And what are you doing now?"

I frown. "I am doing the same."

"Really? Because I've been watching you all for a while, and what I saw from you was your eyes closed and you trying to manifest light without actually doing what you just said you did." Selina stands and comes to stand before me. "Now try it again, but don't close your eyes. Focus on me; make me your target. Start with your mantra of light, and then visualize it radiating from your hands and surrounding me."

I lift my hands. My focus is on Selina as I start to murmur the words linked to light. I then visualize pure white light radiating down my arms, to my hands, and out my fingers. I feel a warmth radiating from my hands. I open my hands wide, visualizing the light strengthening, shining, and then leaving my hands and spiralling around Selina in a beautiful cascade of twinkling light. I visualize the light touching her long white dress, making it sparkle.

"You are doing it," I hear Hope say with a whoop. I close my eyes and lower my arms. Did I do it? Opening them again, I see remnants of light still floating around Selina, a tender smile on her face as she looks at me.

"You see, sometimes it's just changing something and it works." She lifts her hand and strokes a wisp of my long hair behind my ear. "The more you practice, the easier it will get."

"How did it feel?" Vain asks from where she's leaning against the door frame.

"I felt a warmth, nearly like when the sun shines down on you, and a tingling feeling all over my body."

"Now we have a chance of fighting the shadows," Hope says excitedly as she comes to hug me.

"Well, first we need to make sure that is what will keep them back, but remember, keeping shadows back still has them there in the background. We need to find the source of this evil and banish it from Eternity Fae," Selina says seriously.

"If we only knew where they came from or what is happening out there," Love says as she sits on the ground next to Beast. He opens one eye, looks at her, and then closes it again.

"Well, apparently the Fae are stirring. I spoke to Minna today, and she said that some Fae have been complaining. I was going to go speak to Braun today, but I didn't get a chance. I'm thinking of doing it tomorrow." I look at the others. "Maybe you can all go out and speak to your friends and see if they know anything. Like that, we can understand better what we are fighting against."

"That's a great idea. You're not just a pretty face, after all," Vain teases as she comes to stand next to me. I elbow her lightly on her side and smile.

"I'll go speak to the Pixies and the Leprechauns, and if I find any Gnomes on the way, I'll ask them too," Vain says as she strokes her fingers through her beautiful hair.

"I was thinking of going to see my family tomorrow. If any of the Elves are perturbed, they will know," Selina says.

"I'll go talk to the Nymphs, but if I have a guard like apparently we all do now, I suggest he stays behind, because you know how they are," Love says with a wink at us.

"I'll go speak to the Gargoyles, and the Salamanders are close by. Maybe I'll pop in while there," Reality states as she takes a seat next to Selina.

"I guess I have the Witches and the Werewolves," Hope mutters, which has me hiding a smile. None of us like the Witches. Even though they seem nice and stick to what is required, there is always something about them that keeps us on our toes.

"Do you know who is guarding you?" I ask Hope, only to have her smile as she nods.

"Yeah, I got Trek. I guess they know that any other one might not have been able to find me if I wanted, but Trek is amazing. I tried to give him the slip, but he was on me like a flash." As a Werewolf, Trek is one of our best trackers, and Hope can be slippery when she wants to be. She can blend into the vegetation like no one else I have ever seen. Her gift with nature helps her manipulate things around her, which helps when she wants to hide.

"Well, I think I have Zain. He just walked past where I was too many times today for it to be a coincidence," Reality says with a laugh. "I think they all need to learn the art of stealth a little better."

"I don't think Zain could be stealthy even if he tried," Vain quips, which has us all laughing as we think of Zain. As the son of a Gargoyle and an Elf, he is a big, strapping male. He is all strength and brawn, with the magic of the Elves. With his long black hair and bright-blue eyes, he is hard to miss.

"He might be a lug when it comes to hiding, but he's sweet," Reality says with a smile.

"Sweet, is he?" I quip with a raised brow. The girls are always teasing me because of Drez. I think it's time I give them some of their own medicine. I see Reality's cheeks darken with colour as she glares at me. Oh, I think I just hit a nerve. Looks like Reality has the hearts for Zain.

"Don't be silly," she mutters as she looks down at her lap, her hair covering her embarrassed face. I look over at Vain to see her surprised look. Looks like none of us had noticed that Reality has a crush on Zain.

"Well, I still have things to do, so be good," Selina says as she stands to make her way out of the sitting room just as we hear running feet. "What's going on?" she asks as Aqua and Trek rush past the sitting room door. The two men don't answer as they disappear down the corridor towards the back where the kitchen is.

I rush towards the door, only to see Drez and Bain rushing towards the front main door. "Something is happening," Love says as she comes to stand next to me, Beast standing next to her, his fangs showing as he growls low in his throat.

"Stay here," Selina says as she rushes towards the front door where Drez and Bain are standing on each side of the door as if on guard. I see the way the energy around Drez is a static blue as if he's wielding magic. Bain is standing before him; his sword is drawn and at the ready.

My heart races as I hear a noise coming from outside, and then the solid wooden door seems to start budging. "What the hell is going on?" Hope whispers beside me just as Beast turns his head and starts to growl at the windows. I see Reality snap around and lift her fighting staff. All of us have been versed in fighting techniques even though we never thought we would use them. Reality's preference is the staff. I personally prefer the bow, but I don't have mine with me, as I left it upstairs before I went out.

I turn to look at the window and at first don't see anything, as it's pitch dark outside, but then I see something swirling. "What is that?" I ask.

"I think it's the shadows," Love mutters as she pulls her two blades from their holsters at her waist. Since Love started her training, she has had a perchance for blades. She takes her two everywhere she goes, unlike me, who forgets my bow in my room all the time unless I'm training. Well, if it's the shadows, I should be able to drive them back with light, if I can just make enough light to shine outside.

Lifting my hands, I start to envision light radiating from my hands, the mantra I am repeating reverberating through my body, making my whole body tingle. I cannot fail. If this is what is needed to drive them back, then I need to get this right. As soon as I start to envision the light before me radiating down my arms and through my hands, I stretch them out towards the window and imagine it racing out and towards the window, surrounding our home with light.

“I have an idea,” Hope says from behind me. “Surround me with light, too, Dream. I will try to send that light through all the roots to light up the vegetation around us.”

I imagine part of the light shining around all of us and then involving Hope, her skin shining in radiance with light.

“It’s working. I think they are backing off,” Vain says. I hear the haunting sound decreasing in volume, followed by a loud bang. It sounds like it could be the front door, but I cannot stop to look, or the light will stop, and they might come back. Then another crash, and everything becomes deathly quiet.

I continue wielding light, imagining it filtering through the foliage, pushing the darkness back. “You guys are doing it. The trees and plants are shining with a radiant light, and our home is surrounded by light.”

“Dream, are you okay to keep on manifesting for a while longer? I need to get the men to place lights in every window, shining out until daytime.” I nod but try not to break my concentration as I continue imagining the light moving outside. I can feel myself getting tired, but I will hold. I will not let anyone down.

There is movement all around me. I can hear the girls rushing around as they help the men. I wonder how long this will hold them back, as it seems like the shadows are determined to get us. I do not know how long I stand here, manifesting enough light to fight the shadows, before Selina tells me that I can stop. My head is pounding, and I am ready to fall. Manifesting this amount of magic for the time that I did without having done it before exhausted me.

Closing my eyes, I drop my arms. My knees start to give in, but before I can fall, I feel strong arms around me. "Take her to her room. She needs to rest." I feel myself being lifted and held against a strong chest; I am too tired to open my eyes, but whoever is holding me smells so nice that I snuggle up closer.

"Is she okay?" I hear Love ask, concern in her voice.

"She will be fine. She's just exhausted, as she's not used to expelling that amount of energy. Hope, you should also go rest. You two worked wonderfully together."

"I am tired," I hear Hope say, but I do not open my eyes, as I can feel myself drifting off as I am carried upstairs and then placed gently on the bed. I think I hear something being murmured, but I'm not sure as I drift off to sleep.

CHAPTER 5

I'm not sure what wakes me, but my eyes open to the sun shining in through the closed window. I smile as I see the different shades of colour reflecting on my wall as the sun shines on the strips of material hanging from my ceiling. I hear a slight rustle that makes me turn my head to see what it can be. The smile quickly turns into a gasp as I shoot up in bed. Against the far side in my old rocking chair is Drez. He is clearly sleeping and way too big for the chair as it creaks gently every time he breathes.

Last night's attack comes rushing back, and I remember someone carrying me up to bed. Was that Drez? I can feel my cheeks warming with colour as I remember snuggling up to his chest. Looking down at myself, I groan as I see that I am still wearing yesterday's clothes. At least he didn't try to undress me. The thought has my stomach knotting with nerves. Why is he here in my room? Did he stay here to guard me the whole night?

The thought that he might care has me smiling in pleasure. Shuffling back against my headboard, I lean back as I get comfortable to watch Drez sleep. His beautiful long hair falls around his face, his body relaxed in sleep. I wish I had my drawing pad at hand. It would make the perfect portrait, but if I get up to get it, he might wake up. I would rather sit here and be able to stare at him to my heart's content without him knowing than ruin this moment.

I must have been sitting here for over an hour when there is a crash from outside the room as if something tumbled over. I jump in fright and see Drez snap away. His body is off the chair and standing before the bed in seconds. He is here to guard me. How sweet. His muscles are tense, and a blade is in his hand as he stands in a fighting stance.

"I think you can relax; it was most probably Beast knocking something over as he walked past." At my words Drez looks over his shoulder at me.

"You're awake," he mutters.

"Yep, I've been awake for a while."

He turns to face me, a frown adorning his face. "How are you feeling?"

"As fresh as a daisy. Were you keeping an eye on me?"

He nods.

"Thank you, and thank you for bringing me up to bed last night. That is, if I'm right and it was you."

He nods again. "What are you doing today?"

"What?" Does he want to spend time with me? I feel my cheeks heating again as I think of Drez kissing me. I have liked Drez for a long time. Does he perhaps have the same feelings?

"If you are going somewhere, I need to know so that I can be ready. You have been assigned to me."

I swear I feel my heart shattering into a thousand pieces. This is all just a job to him. I am so silly.

"I can take care of myself. Please leave."

He tenses but does not say anything else. Instead, he turns and leaves. As soon as he closes my door, I feel a tear sliding down my cheek. I don't need him following me out of obligation. I will take care of myself. Looking towards my bow, I frown; I am going to need to carry it around with me from now on.

I wipe another tear away; I will not cry. There is too much to do to now feel sorry for myself. We need to be ready to fight whatever is coming for us, and for that, we need to know as much as possible about our enemy.

I am going to go speak to Braun and find out what he knows. After that, I need to train, as I haven't trained in a couple days, and later, when I'm back home, I need to work on my magic. Drez can dawdle his fingers here, because I'm not going to tell him I'm leaving.

After dressing in dark-blue tights and a shimmering blue top, I strap my bow on. Pulling my hair back, I tie it into a ponytail away from my face. Walking towards my bedroom door, I slip out. There is no one around at this early hour, so I make my way downstairs to the kitchen. Walking in, I see Selina. She looks up at my entrance, a smile brightening her expression.

"Morning, Dream. How are you feeling this morning?"

"I'm feeling fine." She frowns at my despondent tone, but no matter how much I try, the thought of Drez wanting to protect me just because it's his job has my mood down in the gutter.

"So, what's bothering you?" she asks as she pushes away the bowl of dried flowers she was working on to make essences and gives me her full attention.

"Nothing, just a lot to do today."

She frowns, knowing I am hiding something, but Selina has her own unique way of making things better without probing for answers.

"Okay then, let me get you some breakfast, and then you can tell me about all these things you have planned for your day." She stands to walk to go prepare my breakfast, but I'm not really in the mood for a big meal and just want to get out of here.

"It's okay, don't worry about breakfast. I'm just going to grab an apple and then I'm off. I want to go speak to Braun while it's still early." Selina turns around and looks at me as I grab an apple from the fruit bowl.

"Be careful out there, Dream. We don't know what is going on yet. Let Drez know you are going out." I walk towards her. Slipping my arms around her waist, I hug her tight. In the absence of our mother, Selina has always been there to guide and take care of us. I have the highest regard for her, but I am not going to let Drez know I'm leaving. He can catch up if he can find me.

Pulling away, I smile before heading towards the back door. Slipping out, I look around, taking in the beauty of the forest at this early hour. Heading towards the trees, I enter the forest, hearing the gentle sway of the trees as the breeze ruffles its leaves, and the rustle of the bushes as insects and animals scurry away.

I head deep into the forest until I reach Braun's home. His oak tree reaches up to the sky, the branches wide and heavy with its foliage, the bark a beautiful vibrant light brown. I frown as I see a deep slash on the bark as I step closer. I see another three, as if claw marks. Who would dare do this to Braun's tree? He must be furious at the abuse of it.

"Braun," I call. "Braun, are you here?" A moment later, I see the shape of Braun stepping from his tree. I start to smile at him, only to gasp as I see that he looks injured. "Oh, Braun, what's wrong?" I rush towards him as he stumbles.

"They tried to poison my tree with their darkness. Braun is not going to let anyone poison his tree." I see the gash on his bark-like body that oozes a dark substance I am sure isn't healthy.

"You are injured; I need to help you." Is it possible that the shadows did this to him? If that is the case, I am going to need the others to try to help him. "Braun, who did this to you?" I hear rustling from the forest, but I do not turn to see as I try to hold Braun up. I see him looking up over my shoulder, but he doesn't tense or flinch, which tells me that it must be some animal being curious.

I start to place my hand over his gash, but my hand is captured by another before I can touch Braun. I turn my head to see Drez standing there, an angry look on his face. "Let go of me. I need to help Braun."

"It is infected. You can't touch the gash, as it will poison you too. It needs to be cleaned like we cleaned Brog's injury first before you can think of healing him."

I huff in anger. "How do you propose I do that without anything here? And why are you following me?" I say, which earns me an angry scowl from him.

"Good thing I am," he mutters, and then he mumbles something, and the radiant blue light that surrounded him yesterday shines on his hands. "This might be uncomfortable, Braun. I'm sorry, but it is needed." He places his hand a few inches away from touching Braun. I see the blue light penetrating the gash. Braun gasps but does not say anything else as his eyes close.

"What are you doing?" I ask as more of the black ooze slips out of the gash.

"I'm cleansing it as much as I can before taking him back home so that Selina can clean it properly." As an Elf, Drez has similar magic to Selina's. Their energy is pure and rich with healing powers; therefore, I do not argue. Instead, I take a step back from Braun so that Drez has more space to work. Placing my arm more firmly around Braun, I try to give him more support, but his weight is starting to drag me down.

"Should I call Selina?" I ask as I see Braun getting weaker.

"No, I will carry him."

I raise a brow. I know Drez is an Elf, and Braun might be thin, but he is solid like his oak tree. Drez won't be able to carry him all the way.

Drez finally pulls back his hands and then looks at me. "Let's go," he mutters as he looks at Braun. He is about to pick him up when Braun shakes his head.

"I will walk. No one is carrying Braun."

"Braun, you're weak. You can't walk all the way," I say as we start making our way back the way I came.

"Braun can walk," he insists. He accepts our support as Drez and I each place one of his arms around our shoulders as we walk, taking most of his weight. To be honest, Braun's weight is tiring me out and I don't know how long I will be able to continue. We are just coming over the last bend when we find Trek and Hope walking towards us.

"What happened?" Hope asks as she rushes towards us, her eyes accessing the damage on Braun's body. "Oh, Braun, they hurt you."

Trek inclines his head for me to step away, which I am more than happy to do, as I am nearly dropping with exhaustion. Trek and Drez quickly make their way towards home, Hope and I following them. I update them on what I know as we walk.

"Selina," I call as we stop before the front door. Only now do I notice the deep grooves on the door from last night's attack.

Selina comes to the door, gasping when she sees Braun between both men. "Quickly bring him inside." At the door, Braun bends his head to get through, as he is taller than anyone else in the house. I wonder where Selina is going to put him, as he won't fit on one of the beds. "In there," she says, pointing towards the sitting room. "Hope, go get my medicines."

When Braun is lying on his back on the floor, Selina kneels beside him, looking at his wound. "You cleansed it?" she asks, looking up at Drez.

"Yes."

She nods before looking back at the wound. "We are going to need the others as we did with Brog. Trek, go get them. Dream, Hope, are you ready? As soon as I have cleaned his wound, I want you to work your magic on him." I move towards Braun's head; Hope kneels on Braun's other side as Selina starts to clean out his gash.

"Now," she says as she finishes.

Instead of closing my eyes like I did with Brog, I keep my eyes open and use the technique I used last night, seeing the light moving through my hands into Braun, through his body until it surrounds the wound. I don't know how long I stand here, trying to expel the darkness from inside Brog. The next thing I know, there are strong hands holding my upper arms as they pull me back.

"Enough, Dream," I hear Drez say from behind me as he continues holding me up. "You have done your part." I look around to see Reality and Love now leaning over Braun. "Come, you need to eat something." Drez guides me out of the room.

"But I need to see how Braun is doing," I mutter.

"Let the others also help him. He will be fine in a couple days," Drez says as we enter the kitchen.

"We have to stop this; they are hurting the forest and everyone in it." I feel the tightness around my heart at the knowledge that whatever is out there isn't just targeting us but everyone in the forest. We will have to come up with a plan to help them.

"We will find a way," Drez says as he walks towards the basket of fruit on the counter

"I need to go see if anyone else is hurt," I mutter, walking towards the back door, but before I can open it, Drez is standing in my way.

"You need to eat."

I look at his hands to find one has grapes and the other has two pears. Lifting my hand, I take one of the pears. "You can get out of my way now," I say as he continues to stand before the door.

"It's dangerous out there," he says as he does not move.

"Were you following me?" Only now do I remember that Drez appeared when I was with Braun after I purposefully left without telling him.

He frowns and then shrugs. "I saw you leaving. You know I am to accompany you when you leave," he says in an accusatory fashion, which has me frowning.

"What if I don't want you following me?" I ask.

"It's my job," he says.

I tense. I am only a job to him. Well, I am not a child anymore, and I don't need a babysitter. "I can take care of myself," I say angrily. I know it's not his fault that I like him, but I don't want him looking out for me as a duty.

"Really? Because if I hadn't come along, you would have touched Braun's wound, and then you would have been infected too." I can feel myself glaring at him as he throws that in my face.

"Are you saying I'm reckless?" I see his surprised look at my question. "Well, let me tell you, I'm not, and if you knew anything about me, you would know that. I don't want you following me anymore."

"Fine, I won't follow you. I will accompany you, but one way or another, when you leave here, I will be with you."

"Argh," I mutter angrily as I snap around and walk away from him, making my way out of the kitchen.

"Where are you going?" he asks from right behind me, which has me stopping abruptly. Looking over my shoulder at his calm face, I glare.

"I told you I'm going out. If you want to follow, that's your problem." And without another word, I make my way out of the house. I can't hear him, but I know he is right behind me, as I can feel his presence. Now that I am outside, I have no idea where I want to go. I just wanted to oppose him. Stepping into the forest, I make my way through the trees, walking aimlessly.

The forest has always been my sanctuary, but now, with everything going on, I feel a restlessness around me that has me on edge instead of at peace. I realize that I am very close to Trollis, a cave where most of the Trolls in Eternity Fae live. Trolls turn to stone in the sun, so they only come out at night and stay inside the cave during daylight hours.

To be honest, I don't usually walk this way, as Trolls aren't the friendliest of beings, but I need to check on as many as I can, and Trolls are one of them.

"This isn't a good idea," Drez suddenly says from just behind me, but I don't pay him any heed, as I'm still upset. To my surprise, I see many of the Trolls outside. Only the guards are usually outside during the day. Walking up to one of the stone statues, I wait until the Troll opens his eyes.

"Why are you all outside?" I ask.

"None of your business, Fairy," he grunts.

"You will answer her," Drez says from right beside me in a voice that brooks no argument. I see the Troll glance at Drez, but then he closes his eyes and does not open them again. Drez lifts his hand as if to prod the Troll, but I stop him.

"It's okay. Let him be," I say as I place my hand on his arm to stop him. "We will look for Toof and speak to him." Toof is the Trolls' leader, and even though gruff and abrupt, he will hopefully listen to me and give me some answers. I can see by Drez's face that he's not happy with letting this Troll to his rudeness, but I'm sure he realizes it will accomplish nothing to upset a Troll, so he soon nods in agreement.

Looking around, I find Toof's statue. "There." I point as I start making my way towards him. "Toof," I call when I am standing before him.

"Why are you disturbing my sleep?" he asks with a frown.

"I'm sorry, Toof, but I have to ask you, have you been having any problems here with any shadows?"

He doesn't answer immediately. "Yes, that is why we are outside."

"Are you saying they are inside?" I ask, looking towards the mouth of the cave where all the trolls live.

"I don't know what it is. All I know is that five of my people have died." I feel my stomach tighten in anger. "Do you know what it is?" he asks. I have always found it strange to talk to a Troll who has transformed themselves into stone, and this time isn't much different, as it's perturbing when you have the Troll looking at you with his stone eyes, the mouth moving but no expression on the stone face.

"We simply call them shadows; we have found that they don't like light. You can fight them by lighting up your cave with as much light as you can manage."

"We don't need light to see," Toof says indignantly.

"Not because of you and your people, Toof, but because of what is attacking you. They don't like light." Toof does not answer for a few seconds, but then he finally agrees to try.

"We have to try to help each other at this time. We still don't know what is manipulating them, so if you find out anything, or if you need any help, please come to us."

Toof simply grunts, which doesn't tell me anything but which I have to accept. I know that Trolls don't like outside help from anyone, but sometimes we need to accept what has been offered to us.

I turn away, feeling deflated even though I was able to give Toof the information needed for him to temporarily conquer the shadows in his home. I am sure it won't solve the problem in the long run.

“This is useless,” I mutter as I start walking away from Trollis.

“Useless?” Drez asks as he steps next to me.

“Yes. Even if they light up their cave, how long will it be before a shadow slips past and gets to another Troll?”

“You have done the best you can with the information we have, at least you have given them a chance. That is something they didn’t have before you came to talk to them.” I stop and turn to look at Drez. What he says is true, and his words appease some of my anxiousness.

“Thank you. I just wish we could do more.”

“We will win this battle yet,” he states with a smile that makes my stomach flutter.

“Yes, but the question is, at the end, who will win the war?”

CHAPTER 6

On our way back home, we come across what seems like a whining noise coming from one of the densest parts of the forest. "What is that?" I ask, covering my ears as the noise seems to penetrate right through my being. Drez doesn't answer, but his hands are also over his ears as he takes a couple steps towards the sound but then stops. Turning towards me, he shakes his head, inclining his head back towards the path home.

I shake my head, wanting to go investigate, but he simply glares at me. I swear he is the most irritating man. "We need to see what it is," I say, screaming the words, but he shakes his head. Huffing, I turn back the way we came and continue making my way home. When I can take my hands from my ears without the sound being overload, I stop and turn towards Drez.

"That sound has never been there before. We need to go see what it is. Maybe that's the cause of these shadows appearing and the portal being closed."

"I will inform Brog. He will send me to come and investigate."

"Are you scared?" I ask sarcastically, which has him glaring at me, but he doesn't answer.

We make the rest of the way home without another word to each other. As we walk in, Drez walks up the stairs towards the rooftop where Brog will be, and I make my way towards the sitting room where Braun was, only to find Shok walking out.

Shok is Gargoyle through and through, but he is the sweetest Gargoyle I have ever met. "How is he?" I ask, only to have him raise his finger to his lips.

"Shhh," he whispers. "Love fell asleep."

I incline my head to look into the room to find Love lying on the couch with a blanket over her that I'm guessing Shok placed there. I look towards Braun still on the ground to find his eyes closed.

Looking back at Shok, I grin. "You're a softy, do you know that?" I tease, only to hear him grunt as he continues on his way out. Instead of going inside, I decide to follow Shok. "There was a strange noise in the forest," I say as we step outside through the back door. Shok stops and looks at me. Only now do I realize that most of the other men are working on the area around the house, placing huge crystal quartz outside. Looking at where they are placing the clear crystal stones, I realize that when the lights are on inside the house they will reflect off the crystals, lighting up the whole area.

"What noise?" At Shok's question, I am brought back to our conversation.

"I don't know. Drez didn't want to go investigate." I place my hands on my hips, looking up at him. "It was never there before, and it's really loud and penetrating. We need to see what it is. We should have gone to see where it comes from."

Shok shakes his head. "It could have been dangerous with you there. I am sure Brog will arrange for us to go see."

I glare at him. "Whose side are you on? I can take care of myself, you know."

His lips turn up, and then he grins at me. "Yep, you are a real warrior," he teases, which has me placing my hands on my hips. "He was just protecting you, squirt." Lifting his hand, he tweaks my nose, using the name he gave me when I was a kid and that he uses when he wants to tease me. I try to smack his hand away, but he's faster than me. "You have to be faster than that," he quips as he turns to make his way towards one of the crystal quartz.

"I'm not a child anymore, you know," I mutter as I follow him, only to have him grin over his shoulder at me.

"Really? I never noticed," he says as he winks at me playfully. Since I was a child, I have always gotten on well with Shok. He has always treated me like an older brother would, and I see him as one. He stops next to Bain, who is turning the quartz to catch the rays of the sun. Bain is our very own Dragon; he is one of the last descendants and a force to be recon with when he gets angry.

"Hi, Bain."

His hypnotic green eyes turn towards me, and he smiles. His long midnight-black hair obscures some of his features as it falls over his face, but it doesn't detract from his rugged good looks. His body, like the other men, is well-toned and big.

"Is this going to work?" I ask as I look at the stone that is half my size. They must have gone this morning into the underground Cave of Life to bring back these crystals, because we never had them before, and the Cave of Life is filled with crystals all over. The energy there is pure and healing.

"It should. If the deterrent is light, then the quartz will do its job until we find a way to get rid of these shadows," Bain says. We are still chatting a couple minutes later when Drez comes outside, followed by Brog.

"Shok, I need you to go with Drez and Zain."

"Are they going to investigate that sound, Brog?" I ask as Shok walks towards where Drez is. I see Zain approaching from the other direction.

"Yes, they are going to try to get closer to it to find out where it is coming from."

"Can I go?"

"No," Drez says before Brog can reply, which has me glaring at him.

"I wasn't asking you," I snap back.

"No, Dream. We still don't know what it is," Brog intercedes.

"What if it has anything to do with the shadows and they need light?" I ask.

"They will be back before it gets dark, so they will be fine," he states as he looks at the three men and then nods at them. I know they are worried about me, but I can take care of myself, and I need to know where that noise is coming from. I turn towards the forest and am about to make my way there, when Brog comes to stand next to me.

"I wouldn't advise it," he says quietly. Looking over at him, I don't say anything, waiting for him to hopefully leave, but he doesn't. "Your sisters and you have a bigger purpose in life than to get killed so soon. Don't be stubborn, Dream. Go practice your magic and see how your powers evolve, as we might need you to be at your strongest sooner than we think."

I sigh. I am being stubborn, and he is right. I need to build up my resistance and my magic. "Fine." I turn, making my way back inside and up to my room. I didn't tell Brog about Toof and his Trolls, but I am sure that Drez has given him a full report of our day. After all, it's only work. I shake my head at the thought and how my heart hurts knowing that Drez doesn't like me. He only sees me as an obligation.

"You're back," Vain says as I walk past her room. I stop, taking a step back to look into her room.

"Yeah, I'm going to go practice to see if I have any more hidden magic somewhere," I mutter.

"Well, I practiced on Love earlier, but now she isn't talking to me," Vain says, looking at me innocently.

My curiosity is piqued. Something must have happened for Love not to talk to Vain. "What did you do?" I ask, only to see Vain grin mischievously, which is never a good sign.

"I worked my magic on her and made her think for a while that she had a shorter leg than the other. Oh, Dream, it was so funny. You should have seen her wobbling around." Vain throws back her head and laughs at her memories of earlier. "Even poor Beast couldn't stop howling at Love's ungainly walk."

"Oh, that's so mean, but don't worry. You know Love. She will be back to her loving self in no time," I say with a smile, only to have Vain shake her head.

"I think she is more upset because Shok was there and he laughed."

"Well, good thing I wasn't here. Like that, she won't be upset at me." Having Shok laugh at her must have been what made Love upset. She has always been more sensitive when comments come from Shok.

"Can I try it on you so we can see how it works?"

I point my finger at her. "No, don't you dare or I'll blind you with light," I warn, which has her raising her hands in defeat.

"Fine, you guys are no fun," she mutters.

"Anyway, I'm going to my room. I'll see what I can come up with," I say as I turn, making my way to my room. Walking in, I approach the bed, sitting down. Just earlier on, I woke up to Drez sitting on the chair, looking out for me. I was so excited and happy thinking that he actually liked me, and then he told me that it was his job. Looking at the painting on my wall, I try to get lost in it like I usually do, finding the peace that the image gives me, but to no avail today, as I'm way too hyped up to relax.

Standing, I walk towards the wall, looking at the waterfall I painted, the water shimmering. Wouldn't it be nice if this magical place was true and behind the waterfall there was an entrance that leads to anywhere a person wants? I can feel myself smiling at my imagination. Closing my eyes, I place my hands on the wall, thinking of how the blossoms around the water smell, the sound of the water falling, the brilliance of the colours all shimmering in my mind. I can even feel splatters of water on my face; that is how strong my visualization is. My hands, instead of feeling the cold wall, are feeling the spray of the water from the waterfall.

I smile as my worries slowly wash away. Opening my eyes, I see the water cascading down before me so beautifully. "What?" I tense, as I am actually seeing water cascading. I snap around, and instead of seeing my room, I see the vegetation of the forest surrounding me. "Oh my, oh no." What did I just do? Did I fall asleep? I pinch myself, only to yelp with the pain. I feel the spray splattering over me as the water cascades down. I know that behind the waterfall is a cavern, but is the cavern the same as I imagined or is it different?

"How do I get back?" My stomach is so knotted in anxiety that I feel sick. "Think, Dream," I say as I look around, seeing everything the same as on the painting that I have on my wall. Does this mean that I can go into any painting that I do, or is it only this one?

Maybe I can paint my way out of here, and then I shake my head at the silliness of my thoughts. "Where are the paints and paintbrushes?" I mutter. I look again at the waterfall. This image has always brought me peace ever since I started to paint it, but now, I'm scared. I look around, finding a boulder. Walking towards it, I take a seat.

I should have painted some fruit too, I think, only to shake my head in exasperation. Looking at the water again, I am hypnotised as the shimmering water seems to cascade all around me like a cascade of different colours. I don't know how long I sit here simply staring at the water, thinking of how I can reverse whatever it is I just did.

Everyone will be so worried when they can't find me, but they might not start to look for me until dinnertime. Brog and the men will most probably think that I disobeyed Brog and went after the men. Will Drez be worried? What will happen if I do not find my way out of here, or how will anyone even know how to look for me here? I feel a tear slip down my cheek. "Oh, Dream, you have done it now."

Maybe I can imagine myself back in my room. Closing my eyes, I imagine my room the way it is, with the bed and the colourful pieces of fabric floating in the breeze from the open window. When I have imagined everything to its last detail, I open my eyes. "No, no, no," I mutter, as I am still sitting on the boulder.

"You're a noisy one, aren't you?" At the sound, I squeak in fright. Jumping up, I look around. Sitting up against a tree is a Leprechaun. His eyes are shut, but he is clearly awake. His high green hat slanted low over his eyes, his reddish-gold beard looking like it could be fluffy to the touch. His green jacket and pants looked slightly wrinkled from sitting on the ground, but besides that, he looks like the typical Leprechaun. I had forgotten that I had drawn one in the picture.

"I'm sorry."

He opens his eyes. "What has you so agitated, Dream?"

"You know me?" How does he know my name? I know that I have never met him before. I see him grin as he nods, and then he jumps up in one fluid motion.

"I know everything about you, child," he states as he walks towards the water. "I know what has been and what is to pass."

I frown. Leprechauns are known to be information brokers, selling the information they've acquired for a fair price. They have a reputation for being tricksters, but they are generally honest, good-hearted people who have a strong regard for honesty.

"If you know what is to pass, are you going to tell me what I have to do to stop the shadows, and how I can get back home?"

He grins as he looks over his shoulder at me. "Well, I might if you pay me."

Argh, I just knew it. "I don't have anything with me to pay you with."

He turns fully to look at me, his expression now serious. "I will tell you everything you need to know; all you have to do is when you get back home, draw next to me my very own pot of gold."

Of course, how did I forget that I could pay him like that? "Fine."

"Okay, then, listen carefully. To beat the shadows, you need to figure out their source and destroy it. Only like that will they go back from where they came from."

"Is that all you have? That is kind of obvious," I mutter.

"Is it obvious that it starts with the sound?" he says as he raises a brow sarcastically. "You know how to conquer the shadows with light.

Now you have to find a way to conquer the repelling sound."

I knew that sound had to have something to do with what was happening. I wonder what they found? I need to get back to tell them that we need to stop the sound.

"But remember, the sound is a means used and not the source. To win this war that has been waged against all of you, you will have to find the source, and only then will we be free again."

"What's the source?"

"If I knew what the source was, I wouldn't have told you that you had to find it, now would I?" he says with a shrug.

"Okay, you have answered one of my questions. Now for the other one." I really need to get back now that I know that we need to stop the sound.

"You know the answer to that one. Now think, what were you imagining when you walked into your painting?"

I close my eyes, thinking back. What did I imagine?

“I don’t k . . .” I start to say, but as I open my eyes, I see that he has gone. I start to wander around the pool of water, seeing the path that leads up behind the waterfall, and then suddenly I remember what I was thinking when I was touching the painting. Rushing up the embankment, I slip a few times, but I finally make it behind the waterfall. My heart is racing. If this does not work, then I might be stuck here forever. “Please, please let this work.”

The darkness of the cave surrounds me, the sound of the rushing water behind me crashing down into the pool. There is nothing but darkness. Am I mistaken? Closing my eyes, I imagine my room, the window open, the sound of the birds outside, the breeze blowing around me. I hear the sound of the others moving around the house as they go about their day. Wait . . . the sound of the others? Opening my eyes, I whoop. I am back. I was so scared that I would never get back.

CHAPTER 7

"Oh, my word, where have you been? Do you know how worried we have all been?" Vain says when she sees me walking past her room. I stop and turn just in time as she comes barrelling against me, hugging me close.

"What do you mean?"

She pulls back to glare at me, "You have been gone for two days, where have you been?" Two days have gone past since I entered the painting, how is it possible? While I was there it felt like only hours.

"In my painting" I state distractedly

"What? What do you mean your painting?" I see her frown as she takes a step back, her eyes roving over my body. "and you are still wearing the same clothes you were wearing when you disappeared." I look down at my black tights and dark red tunic.

"Dream!" Love calls as she looks out of her bedroom and then she is running towards us.

Her arms are around me and she is hugging me close kissing my cheek. “You here, oh I was so worried.” She says and then she is stepping back, “Did the men find you?” there are so many questions and I haven’t even started to answer Vain’s ones.

“No, and I wasn’t gone” at my reply they both frown

“Well, I beg to differ” Vain says as she places her hands on her hips, “we have looked all over the place and trust me, no one could find you. The men have been out searching, Drez is out of his mind thinking it’s his fault.”

“What?” why would Drez think it’s his fault?

“I’m serious, remember when I walked past your room and told you that I was going to practice magic?” Vain doesn’t reply but nods, “well, I was touching my painting one minute and the next I was in it” at my statement both of them stare at me with a surprised look on their faces.

“Are you saying that this whole time you have been in your wall?” I glance back when I hear Hope’s voice, Reality standing next to her on the landing to the stairs a suspicious look on her face.

"Not my wall, but my painting" I say, "I closed my eyes thinking about how the water would feel on my skin, how I could hear the birds chirping and the next moment when I opened my eyes I was standing in my painting."

"You mean that you went into that waterfall painting you have on your wall?" Love asks in surprise

"Yes, and it was just like it too except real, but I was so scared that I couldn't get back." At that hope takes my hand and Love hugs me again.

"I wonder If you would be able to take all of us there if ever needed or if only you can go" Reality says with a pensive look on her face.

"I can try, but first I need to eat as I am starving." I say, "apparently I haven't eaten in two days." with that I turn to go back down the stairs only to encounter Brog rushing upstairs when he sees me, he stops.

"Girl, where the hell have you been?" when Brog calls any of us girl we know that we in trouble.

"she was stuck in her painting, how awesome is that?" Vain says as she comes to stand next to me, she continues to explain to Brog what I just told them. He looks from her to me a suspicious look on his face.

"Why did you stay there for two days?" he asks

Shrugging "It felt like only hours while I was there, I swear I didn't know I could do that, or I would be more prepared."

"Why, what happened?" he asks with a frown

"It's just that I didn't know how to come back once I was there, if it wasn't for the Leprechaun I might have taken longer."

"There was a Leprechaun?" Reality asks

"Yes, and he told me something else." I say looking back at Brog, "what did the men find when they went looking for the sound that Drez and I heard?" at that Brog scratches at his stubble and shrugs.

"They weren't able to get close to whatever is making that sound, and when they got back we couldn't find you so we haven't been back every since then because all the men have been out looking for you." He shakes his head suddenly, "In the painting," he mutters as he turns, "next time must remember to look in the artwork." He glances over his shoulder at me and inclines his head for me to follow. "Why are you asking about the sound?" when I draw next to him he places his arm around my shoulders and squeezes gently.

“Don’t ever give us a fright like that again.” He states a smile pulling at his lips

“I’ll try not too” I murmur as we start making our way downstairs, “when I was speaking to the Leprechaun, he said that the shadows start with the sound.”

“I told you guys” Hope says as they follow Brog and I

“Dream,” Selina calls as she rushes towards us, “I thought it was your voice I heard” she pulls me towards her holding me close, “Oh child you had us so worried” she murmurs against my hair and I can hear the deep emotions as her voice cracks.

“I’m okay, sorry to worry you” Love starts relating what happened while Brog leads me to the kitchen.

“Oh, my poor angel, you must have been so scared” Selina says as she makes her way in her calm and collected way towards a pot that is sitting on the stove. “Take a seat I will feed you; your mother would never forgive me if we lost you.”

“Did the Leprechaun say anything else?” Brog asks as he takes a seat at the table next to me.

“he said that we need to find the source to end this war, that the sound is just a venue for the shadows.” Selina places a plate of food before me as the others start commenting around the table about what I have just disclosed.

“Maybe if we can find out where the sound is coming from, we can figure out what the source is” Vain says

“Or who the source is” Reality states

“The problem still remains that the sound is so piercing that we can’t get close to it.” Brog comments with a frown.

“Is there nothing we can place over our ears that will stop us from hearing the sound?” Hope asks

“Drez and I were covering our ears to try and get close to it and I promise you it is so excruciating that you feel your whole body vibrating with the sound, just covering your ears won’t work. You would need to be deaf not to hear it.” I state thinking back to when Drez and I heard it.

“Imagine the poor Fae that live in the vicinity of that sound, no mellow soothing bird songs for them now.” Vain says which has me dropping my fork as I remember something that the Leprechaun said, which has everyone turning to me at the sound.

“What you said just made me remember something the Leprechaun mentioned, he spoke about repelling sound and before that he spoke about how the light combated the shadows, so what is to say that soothing calm music won’t combat repelling sounds” at my comment everyone sits for a few seconds just looking at me, I can tell that they are contemplating my theory.

“It is worth a try, and it makes sense” Selina says as she too takes a seat at the table.

“But how would we know what calm music to play?” Vain asks with a frown

“We don’t need to know do we?” Brog says as he looks over at Love, “Your voice sooths and calms those around you when you sing Love and you make up your own lyrics every time, what if all that is needed is Love to sooth with her voice?”

Love looks at us with a surprised look on her face, then she looks back over her shoulder at beast that followed us downstairs and is now laying at the foot of the table. “Do you think that is all that it will take?” she asks

“All we can do is try” Selina says just as we hear the door open and voices approaching, then Zain and Trek enter the kitchen stopping in their stride when they see me.

“You found her” Zain says as a smile splits his face

“I told you I sensed her here” Trek mutters as he walks towards me, stopping besides my chair I see his nostrils flare and I know that he is scenting where or with who I have been.

“I’m going to go and tell the others and especially Drez before he destroys the whole forest.” Zain comments as he makes his way out the back door.

“What is going on?” I ask looking at Love as Brog and Selina explain to Trek what happened.

“What happened is that Drez blames himself for you going missing. He said that it was his responsibility to keep you safe and he didn’t.” she leans in closer in a conspirator fashion, “You should see, he was so distraught from what I have heard he has hardly slept in the two days going out first light and coming back because the others force him to. And now from what

Trek just said sounds like your Drez is turning the forest upside down to find you."

"He's not my Drez" I mutter, but my heart is racing at the thought that maybe I am more to him than just an obligation.

"Really? Maybe someone should tell him that because he sure was acting like he would destroy anyone that hurt you." There is a dreamy look in Love's eyes as she talks.

"You just imagine romance everywhere Love, its just a job for him" I mutter feeling that fluttering of hope in my stomach at the thought that maybe, just maybe he might like me like I like him.

"If you say so" Love states as she sits up straight and smiles one of her conspirator smiles.

"What are you up to?" I ask but she shrugs an innocent look on her face.

"Dream" I glance towards Selina realizing that she must have called my name before, but I was distracted with Love that I did not hear her. "You know what this means don't you?" I frown at her question. She must realize that I am completely unaware of what she is saying because she gives me one of her maternal smiles and shakes her head.

“It means that you have found another of your gifts” she leans forward stretching out her hand she takes mine and squeezes gently. “You can paint anything you want and then enter the painting, in this case because of your foresight even though you didn’t know it at the time when you painted the Leprechaun it worked to helped us in this fight that we find ourselves in.” I smile, I hadn’t thought about it that way but now that she mentions it, it does make sense. I will have to think very carefully next time before I make a painting and make sure that I always make a way out and that there will always be something to help me if need be.

Suddenly there is a crash which has me jumping in fright as I look back towards the kitchen door that has been thrust open. Drez is standing there in the doorway, his chest moving up and down as he takes in deep breaths. His eyes are a bright blue which they usually go when Eldrin’s are in combat, and they are focused on me. I can feel myself tensing, turning fully in my chair I face him as he finally approaches, his eyes don’t deviate from mine as he draws closer.

“Drez” Brog calls but to no avail as he comes to stand before me.

"Where were you?" his voice is low as if he is finding it difficult to get the words out.

"In my painting" he frowns so I continue by explaining to him what happened, his body continues tense as I come to the end of my telling.

"Never do any of that if I'm not around to protect you again" by his tone I can see that it would not be prudent to deny him this request. I have never seen Drez like this before, he isn't much of words instead missioning on and doing what he has to do without forcing the situation but in this case I can tell that he will not be appeased unless I confirm that I will be adhering to his wishes. "Do you hear me?" he asks when I do not reply immediately.

"Yes" his eyes travel over my body as if confirming that I am unharmed before he turns and leaves as abruptly as he entered.

"Yikes" Vain murmurs from where she's sitting, "that was intense"

"What were you saying earlier on about Drez not being yours?" Love whispers as she leans towards me. I know that I am looking perplexed, but I never thought to see Drez in such a fury and especially because of me. Is it possible that Love is right and Drez does care about me more than he professes?

CHAPTER 8

When I finally make my way upstairs, I am surprised to see that Drez has made himself comfortable in my room by placing a mat on the ground before the painting on my wall and is fast asleep. What is he doing here? I cannot go to sleep with him just a couple feet away from me. Frowning, I grab a turquoise nighty and am making my way towards the bathroom, when I tense at his sleepy voice.

“Where are you going?”

“To bathe, and what are you doing here,” I ask, turning towards him fully.

“Making sure you don’t disappear again. From now on, we stay together.”

“You’re not comfortable there on the floor. If I promise to always tell you from now on when I go out, will you go sleep in your own room?” Drez sits up on his makeshift bed. I see that he has placed his sword next to him for easy access. Two other blades have been placed near his head. *Is he expecting something to come charging out of the painting?* I think sarcastically.

"No, as it seems that even at home, you have a tendency to get into trouble," he mutters as he frowns at me. "Now are you going to go bathe or stand there the whole night?"

I tense. *Argh, irritating man.* Turning, I hurry into the bathing room. I should go sleep somewhere else just to spite him, but I know I am not going to, as I am tired and really need a good night's sleep.

Turning on the water in the bath, I let it run, seeing the semi-precious stones that adorn it shining in the reflection of the water. I love being able to lie back in the bath and let the water sooth all my worries away, but today, knowing that Drez is just a few steps away has me hurrying through what is usually a long, relaxing process for me.

When I am done, I make my way towards my bed, not once looking towards where Drez is lying, but I have the suspicion that he is asleep and not bothered with my show of anger. I touch the stone around my neck, thinking of the time that it used to warm when someone needed calming when having a nightmare. Ever since the problems started, my stone has been still.

Closing my eyes, I think back to everything that has happened and how a couple days have changed me. Before, I was naïve without a care in the world, going about my normal routine, not thinking of what evil is out there. Now all I can think about is how I will make Eternity Fae safe again for those around me. I thought growing my magic would only come with time, but now that I have started to see that the power is all in me and all I need to do is unleash it, I find myself more confident in the Fairy that I am and the Fairy I will one day become.

I must have drifted off to sleep, because the next thing I know, there is smoothing wet on my cheek. I turn my head, but then it moves to my forehead. Opening my eyes, I see a big tongue coming straight for me again. "Argh," I squeal as I hurriedly try to get out of Beast's reach.

"Beast," I snap, only to see a smiling Love standing by the door of the room.

"Sorry, did he wake you?" I glare at her as she approaches, her eyes twinkling in amusement.

"Not funny, Love," I mutter as I rub at my face.

"Well, sorry, but everyone is getting ready and you are sleeping the day away," she says as she comes to sit at the bottom of my bed.

"Getting ready for what?" I ask with a frown. Were we supposed to go somewhere today?

"To go find the sound that is the cause of these shadows that have been plaguing Eternity Fae," she says as she flickers her hair back over her shoulder.

"We are going there now?" I jump out of bed as I ask the question. Looking around, I see my bow against the wall where I left it yesterday when I appeared again in my room. I quickly find myself tights and a long-sleeve black T-shirt with silver threads intwined in the black that twinkle as I walk. I change into the clothes and then plait my hair so that I can keep it out of the way in case we come up against something unexpected.

"Brog thought best that we try to find the source of the sound sooner rather than later, as we don't know what it does."

"Who's all going?" I ask, only now realizing that Drez is no longer in the room. So much for keeping an eye on me.

"Hope, you, me, and some of the men. Reality and Vain went to check on some of the Fae we haven't yet seen." I want to ask her if Drez is coming, but I hold my tongue, knowing that Love will use that to tease me. Sliding my feet into my high leather boots, I walk over to my bow. Picking it up, I slide it over my shoulder as I tie it in place.

"I'm ready," I state as I start making my way towards the bedroom door.

"You haven't told me yet how it was yesterday after you came to bed," Love asks as she falls into step.

"Nothing to say," I murmur. Glancing at her, I see her raise a brow at my answer.

"I know that Drez slept in your room last night. I saw him sneaking away this morning," she says as she elbows me playfully in the side.

"Yes, he slept on the floor, and he was sleeping when I went to bed and gone this morning, so you see, snoopy, there is nothing to tell." We arrive downstairs to see Hope having an argument with Trek. Her hands are on her waist as she glares at him.

"Don't be stubborn," Trek says, only to have Hope shooting him a murderous look.

"Look who's talking. You are the king of stubbornness," she shoots back.

"This isn't a joke, Hope. Just wear something sensible."

I look at what Hope is wearing and smile. Guess her skimpy little shorts do not agree with his sensibilities.

"And what, may I ask, is sensible for you? Armour?" she asks sarcastically.

"Do you have any?" he asks with a raised brow, and it seems he is contemplating it.

"Argh," she mutters.

"Morning," I say loudly. Trek turns his head to look at us and then points.

"See, look how they dressed. Can't you put something like that on?" Hope glances at us and then back at him.

"You're not my father, you know," she says angrily before she turns and makes her way out the front door.

"Stubborn woman," Trek mutters as he follows her.

"Well, looks like this will be an interesting group," Love quips with a smile. "Here comes

Drez." My head snaps around towards the kitchen, and I see him approaching, his eyes roaming over my body before he finally meets my eyes.

"Morning, Drez," Love greets as she hurries past him towards the kitchen, leaving me alone with him, the rascal.

"Morning," he replies, but his eyes do not leave mine. "How did you sleep?"

"So well that I didn't even hear you snore."

He frowns. "I don't snore."

"Are you sure?" I quip as I turn to make my way outside, hearing him sigh as he follows me.

"Here." Looking over my shoulder, I see him holding out a fig bag. Turning, I stop and take the bag that has been made out of fig leaves and dried out with a special oil to harden them so that they don't tear when it is stitched together with fine silk sourced from the silk worms. Looking inside, I smile; he has filled it up with fruit.

"Thank you." He nods but does not comment as he looks over his shoulder as Love and Shok walk out the door with Beast following them.

"How far is it from here?" Love asks as they join us.

"It's about an hour's walk," Trek says as he and Hope join us. I see Hope is still wearing her shorts, and Trek looks less than pleased. One thing he will find out about Hope is that she is as stubborn as a mule and nothing changes her mind unless she wants to change it.

"What happened when you went to find it before?" I ask as we make our way through the forest. Trek and Drez are leading the group, with Shok at the back.

"We tried to go as close as possible, but the sound is excruciating. We had to give up after a while."

"Do you have a plan today?" Hope asks.

"We try to get as close as possible and then get Love to start singing. We are hoping that the sound of her voice will start to drive that sound into itself. We also noticed that the vegetation is very dense when we were trying to approach. That is where you come in, Hope," Shok replies.

"Looks like you just came along for the walk," Love quips as she pokes me in the shoulder. I look back at her and pull a face, which has her grinning.

“No, we noticed that through the vegetation, it was really dark. Maybe as Hope moves the vegetation, it will brighten, but if not, we will need Dream to light the way.”

“You hear that?” Love quips. “You are lighting the way, Dream.”

“You’re full of chirps today, aren’t you?” I state, grinning at her playful mood.

“We must be getting close,” Hope interrupts. “I can feel the earth’s agitation.”

Thinking back, I’m not surprised. If that sound penetrates the earth like it was penetrating us, then everything around that area must be dying with the spiked vibrations it transmits.

“Is it my imagination, Drez, or is the area that the sound is reaching growing?” Shok asks as we start hearing a faint sound in the distance.

“It’s growing,” Drez replies as he stops. “Love, you should start wielding your music spell.”

“Okay, I really hope this works,” she says before she closes her eyes for a minute before she starts humming.

“Listen, everyone, listen to the whisper of Love.
Let your hearts open to the brightness that explodes within,

Let your souls float in a pink sea of promise,
A sea of caring, of heart-warming goodness
That radiates around you.
Let your inner light shine, shine, shine.
Let your inner light shine, shine, shine."

Love's song has me feeling relaxed and good, I can feel my heart beating to a tune of love, of peace. Her mellow tones penetrating the path that we walk, everything that was looking dreary and glum before is starting to radiate with life. I know that it's a perception, but that perception grows, and so does the vibration of love inside each one of us and in each one of the beings that might be able to hear her right now. That love will grow and fight the darkness starting to eat away at everything in its path.

"Listen, everyone, listen to the whisper of Hope.
A whisper that can grow and flourish,
That can bend and twist but never break.
Open your mind to the hope that lies within,
Hope that will radiate and shine, shine, shine.
Hope that will radiate and shine, shine, shine."

The sound is becoming louder as we approach. The only thing we have to guide us is the level of the sound. As Shok explained, the vegetation is becoming denser, and I notice the light is becoming obscured in certain parts. "Let's stop here," Trek says as he looks back at us. "Love, you carry on singing, but here, sing into this, as you might need it." I see Trek handing Love what looks like a horn. She frowns at him but doesn't hesitate as she lifts it to her mouth and sings.

The sound is projected out louder and wider into the forest. The horn somehow works as a microphone, increasing the volume of Love's voice.

"Listen, everyone, listen to the whisper of Dream.
Let all your dreams develop and blossom.
Believe in your dreams, believe in yourself.
Expand your horizon and live your dream.
Dreams that will thrive and shine, shine, shine.
Dreams that will thrive and shine, shine, shine."

Love continues to sing her lyrics, her eyes closed as she feels everything around her, singing to the Fae who can hear her, to the animals, plants that can feel the love radiating in her words. Hope is on her knees, her hands flat on the ground as she sends life and light through the earth to brighten our path and revive that which is losing its energy.

What should I do to help? As soon as the thought enters my mind, I see myself sending light around me, filling the forest with brightness to diminish the darkness that has befallen it. Stretching out my arms, I visualize the light shining through my body, running through my veins, down my arms, and out through my hands, but suddenly, something flies straight into me. Before I can protect myself, it has knocked me off my feet and flat on my back. I lay here stunned as I see Drez suddenly standing above me like an avenging god, his sword shining the same magnetic blue as his eyes. His body is tense and ready to fight, daring the enemy to attack, and instead of being frightened of what is out there, I feel safe, because I know that he will die before he lets anything happen to me.

CHAPTER 9

"What was that?" Shok roars, and then all hell breaks loose. "Duck." I was just about to sit up, when I feel Drez's weight on me.

"Stay down," he mutters.

"What is it?" I ask, trying to see past his bulk but only seeing wisps of something flying around, and then from above, I see it. It looks like a deformed bird of some kind. The dark wings are longer, and it seems to have tiny teeth, and the eyes are a dark red. Lifting my hand, I visualize the light radiating out and shining on the creature. As soon as the light touches it, there is a shrill sound, and then it explodes into tiny little particles.

"Move, Drez," I say, but he does not budge. Instead, he pushes me back down.

"Let me up. I can make it stop." But he ignores me. "Argh," I mutter. If he does not let me do it one way, I will do it another. I take hold of his hand that is holding his sword as he swings every time one of those things gets too close.

"What are you doing?" he asks as I see the light moving through me into him. Suddenly, his sword lights up like a beacon, the blue so radiant that I hear the ear-piercing screeches of the creatures before there is absolute quiet.

"Wow," Hope gasps, shading her eyes as she sits up once Trek gets off her. Drez looks down at me, a strange look in his eyes as he slowly helps me to sit up.

"You can stop now," he says, which has me frowning, as I am not casting any longer.

"I'm not doing anything." I pull my hand away from his, and the light slowly starts to dim.

"Try it again without using your gift. Just touch his hand again while he's wielding his sword," Love says from where she is standing before Shok. I frown but lift my hand and touch his again, feeling him tense, but he does not move away. Immediately, the light around his sword starts to strengthen and shine. I look up at his face to see him looking down at me instead of at his sword, a look that penetrates my very soul.

"I knew it," Love says. "You two enhance each other's powers."

I pull my hand away again, feeling my cheeks flush in embarrassment.

"Well, at least now we know how to cast the light," Trek says as he pulls a leaf out of Hope's hair. She lifts her hand and slaps his away as she glares at him, clearly still upset with him.

"Listen," Shok says suddenly. "Can you hear that?" I frown, trying to hear something, but the only thing I can hear is the faint sound of what we are searching.

"Hear what?" Love asks as she looks up at Shok.

"It's softer," Drez mutters.

"Yes, it's softer, which means it's working," Shok says as he looks around at all of us. "We need to continue, but with caution, as I think we might have some more surprises."

"Stay close to me," Drez says as Trek and Hope make their way to the front of the group. Love and Shok are behind us. Love starts to sing while Hope opens a path for us with her powers. I lift my hands, shining my light around the vegetation; that is, until I feel Drez placing his hand that is holding his sword in mine. The light that I was shining intensifies and brightens, showing every hollow and groove in the forest before us. We can hear scurrying from ahead, as if whatever was lying in wait decided to run away.

It is a slow trek, as the vegetation gets denser with each step we take. As soon as Hope pushes the vegetation back, it starts to grow back faster, and the sound is growing louder. "This isn't working," Hope says after another few steps, and we can see how exhausted she is from constantly using her gift to control the vegetation around us.

"There must be another way," I murmur as I hear Love's voice break. Looking back, I see Shok nudge her as he hands her water to drink.

"If you think of something, I'm all ears," Hope murmurs.

I look up at Drez to see him looking around, a frown on his face. "What's wrong?" I ask.

"There is something following us," he mutters as he inclines his sword to his left, shining the light in the area. Immediately, there is scuttling, evidence that there is something following us.

"What if we join our gifts like I am doing with Drez? Maybe like that it will be stronger and quicker," I suggest. If we can expand each other's gifts, then we should be able to proceed at double the speed we are now.

"I'm up to try anything," Hope says as she stops, waiting for me to join her. "So how are we going to do this?"

"I'm not sure," I murmur. Now that I'm next to her, I have no idea how we can proceed so as to increase the reach of our powers.

"Try to do what you did with Drez," Trek says as he stands with his back to us, his eyes on the foliage around us, looking for any unsuspecting attacks.

"That might work. Remember when the shadows attacked us at home and we cast light into the darkness, you through the earth to the plants and trees?" I ask.

"Yes, that will work," Hope says as she places her hand in mine.

"Love, maybe the music can flow through us. That will have the energy of the song filtering through the plants and the earth, reaching the source of the sound sooner." Love inclines her head but then nods as she comes to stand on my other side to hold my hand.

"Well, here goes nothing. One, two, three." I can feel the energy flowing through me. It's like little electrical pulses flowing through my veins. The sound of Love's voice washes through my body like silk against my skin. Hope's energy revitalizes me, giving me a fresh boost to face what awaits us. We start making our way forward instead of stopping every few steps like we were doing. The path seems to open for us.

"It's working," Trek says just as something comes flying towards us, but Trek lifts his arms, catching the boulder in the air before it can crash into us.

"On guard," he yells as another one from the other side comes crashing towards us, but Shok stops this one with his battle-axe.

"Oh no they don't," Hope mutters, and suddenly there is a heave in the ground. "Hear me now, find those who wish us harm and detain them with your roots and branches." Another boulder comes flying towards us, but then there is a gurgling sound and thrashing, as if whatever is out there is fighting against restraints.

"I'm going to see what it was," Drez says as he starts making his way towards one of the sounds.

"No," I call, but he does not hear me as he continues into the brush.

"Let's carry on. He will catch up," Trek says as he walks on.

"No. What if there is something else out there?" I look over my shoulder at Shok. "Shok, please go with him."

"Sorry, sweetness. I need to make sure nothing comes at the three of you from behind." He gives me a tentative smile as he searches the woods. "Don't worry, he can take care of himself." I reluctantly continue our trek forward, but I periodically look back to see if he is approaching. After walking for a while, I finally hear footsteps and see him coming out of the trees towards us. Silly man, placing himself in danger unnecessarily and without any backup.

As soon as I see that he is fine, I ignore him, instead looking forward and making sure that my energy penetrates the darkness and enhances my sisters. The sound has remained at a doable decibel. I know that is because of us, and if anything, it has quietened but hasn't stopped. After walking for another ten minutes or so, we encounter burnt and broken trees and bushes. I hear Hope's gasp of pain when she sees the dead trees and the trampled and burnt foliage in our path.

"We are getting close," Drez states as we come across a dead deer that has been torn apart by what looks like claws. I feel my stomach tightening at the sight of the poor thing. It did not even have a chance. The unnecessary violence makes me sad at the evilness that is evident.

"Do you think the shadows did this?" I ask as we walk past the poor thing.

"Maybe. It looks like the claw marks that Brog had when he was attacked," Trek says. The sound here is more intense, and we are starting to feel it vibrating through our bodies, but it's still not as bad as when I first heard it with Drez.

"I know where we're going," Shok suddenly says. "Dream, do you remember that cave we used to hide in when we were young?" I look around to try to get my bearings. With everything around us dead and grey, it is difficult to see where we are, but when he mentions the cave, I look around with a new perception. It has been so many years since I have been here that I'm not certain.

"I remember, but with everything in such a poor state, I'm not sure where we are."

"I think the source of this sound might be in there. Remember how the sound reverberated in that cave?" I smile, remembering those times so long ago.

"Isn't that the cave where you tried to kiss her?" Hope asks as she swipes her free hand to the right. Immediately, the roots and stumps of a dead tree that was in our path starts to retract.

"What?" Drez asks as he stops and turns to look at Shok, a scowl on his face. "You kissed her?" He takes a step towards Shok as if to confront him, but I can't see what happens, as Shok is behind me and I can't exactly turn around when Hope and Love are both holding my hands.

"No, no, I didn't," Shok states. "Swear, I didn't touch her."

I hear Hope laugh and know that she is purposefully teasing Drez. Love elbows me in the side. When I turn to look at her, she winks as if to say *I told you so*.

"No lack of trying," Hope says, looking behind us, a grin splitting across her face.

"Thanks, Hope, you're a real friend," he mutters, which has me grinning at his sullen response. I remember that day when we were in the cave and Shok walked up to me, stating that he thought we should kiss just to see how it was. At that age, I had other ideas and kneed him before running away. He was so angry at me that he did not speak to me for a whole week. I see Drez out the corner of my eye. Looking over at him, I see his eyes are on Shok, and he looks far from friendly.

Looks like Love might be right and Drez does have feelings for me. I am so distracted that I only realize there is danger when we are nearly upon it. Trek, Shok, and Drez push the three of us into a circle as they stand with their backs to us. "Six is better than three," I mutter as a crazy thought enters my mind.

"What?" Hope asks loudly so she can be heard above the intense sound. There are four hooded figures at the end of the path. Their faces are darkness itself, the hoods low, covering half their faces or what should be their faces. They are huge and much taller than Shok, who is the tallest of the three men. The dirty black threads of their capes hide the bodies below.

"Turn, touch the men. One hand on them and the other on one of us." I let go of their hands and turn to show them what I mean. My right hand rises, and I place it flat against his back, and then with my left hand, I place it on Love's upper arm.

Love nods and copies my actions, the same with Hope. The men don't show any sign of our touch on them, but I for one can feel Drez's muscles tensing under my touch.

"There are three, Love, Hope, and Dream,
The heart, the soul, and the mind.
All are here; we are a trinity.
Let the Fae energy surround us,
Let the earth bind us,
And let our hearts guide us."

I repeat Love's words, and then Hope joins in and repeats the words. An amethyst light twirls around our group, and I know that the energy of our trinity has been linked to fight this danger. The hooded figures howl as if banshees, and then they rush towards us. I feel my heart beating erratically, thinking that maybe I should have grabbed my arrows instead of using our energy, but what possible damage would our weapons have against these creatures?

Whatever the source of the sound is, these creatures are the product of it. Drez swings his sword, trying to stop the creature attacking him. Trek is fighting with two long blades, his wolf very much evident as he growls at them. His muscles strain as he wields the blades, slashing continuously, trying to wound them. Shok has his own unique way of fighting. His axe befalls the two fighting him at the same time as his flesh turns stony, impeding them from wounding him.

"They are too strong!" Hope screams to be heard over the fight. She is right; it does not seem like the men's weapons are doing any kind of damage to these creatures. I see roots popping out of the ground, and I know that Hope is trying to detain them so that we have a better chance of stopping them, but to no avail. Unlike whatever the other creatures were, these are too quick and strong for the roots to get a chance to hold them still for any number of times.

"We can't hold them back for much longer," Trek growls as the creature rips a gash down his arm. Drez is having the same difficulty. I see various wounds on his body. These things are tiring them down. What are their intentions? Well, let me see what I can do. They are a figment of evil, so the only way to beat them is to fight evil with good. Closing my eyes, I draw everyone's energy to me, feeling a rush of power overflow every fibre of my being.

"You want to fight us? Well, fight this!" And then instead of lighting everything up, I enter the darkness that is their beings. I can feel the oppressive darkness and evil clawing at me as I penetrate their evil energy and start filling it with goodness. Taking Love's unique goodness and Hope's power of life and my power of inner light, I fill these evil creatures with every fibre of pure energy that I can.

I feel my mind swirling, my body getting heavier, but I don't stop until I am sure they are forever gone. I hear the others screaming my name, but I don't stop until there is only light and the darkness has completely dissipated.

I feel a weakness within myself and know that I have used every fibre of magic that I am capable of. My head is swirling with a purple light flashing around and around in my mind behind my eyes. My body feels like it is falling, but it never touches the ground as it continues to fall. The others' voices become distant. I try to open my eyes, but they are weighed down by the swirling motion, as if I'm in a whirlwind, and then all of a sudden, everything goes still and the swirling purple light starts to disappear.

I hear many voices all at once, sounds that I have never heard before. Opening my eyes, I tense. Where am I? My heart starts to race, my stomach knotting. "Where are we?" I turn my head to encounter Love next to me, a look of horror on her face as she looks around.

"Dream, where did you bring us?" Hope asks from behind us. Turning, I encounter the other four all looking around. I am relieved to know that they are all fine and we are together.

"We are in the city," Drez says, his eyes coming back to look at me. "You have brought us into the city." All the men who protect us have at one time or another been outside of Eternity Fae and among the humans, as it is part of their training, but Hope, Love, Reality, Vain, and I have never been allowed here.

"This is horrible," Hope says as she looks around at the concrete buildings that we can see in the distance. "There is hardly any life here." With that, she is clearly meaning nature, and I agree with her. Looking at where we are standing, I frown. What is this place? There is a long contraption with metal wheels to one side. The wheels seem to run on metal tubes.

“Can you get us back?” I look up at Drez, and even though I wish I could say yes, I have no idea how I even got us here. My head is still feeling heavy, and my body, lethargic. Even if I wanted to, I doubt I have even a drop of magic in me.

“I don’t know,” I murmur before everything starts to go dark and I once again feel myself falling, but this time, I feel strong arms holding me, and I know that I am safe.

CHAPTER 10

I don't know how much time has passed, but when I finally open my eyes, I am lying on some sort of padded seat. Turning my head, I see square windows and the roof is low and rounded. "You're finally awake." Looking towards the opposite side of where I am lying, I see Love leaning back against the side of her seat. Her legs are bent, and her feet are resting before her.

"Hey." I sit up, feeling my head dip but then normalize. "What happened?" I ask, looking around.

"You fainted, so everyone thought it best that we wait here until you are well again. Are you okay?"

"Yes, I'm feeling much better. Where is everyone?"

"Drez went looking for food and to find out where we are. Trek and Hope went to look for clothes, as apparently we can't walk around in these."

"I'm sorry, Love, that I got us into this predicament." I feel bad that we are all in this awful place and it is all my fault.

"No, don't be sorry. You know that if you hadn't gotten us out of there, we would have been dead. I have been thinking, in a way, it's good, as maybe we can find out what is going on and why we have been closed out from the rest of the Fae." Love turns. Dropping her feet to the ground, she faces me. "Just think, Dream, we can contact Mom and Dad and get them to send help. They will know what those shadows are and maybe what or who is doing it."

"I had not thought about that, but the idea does have merit." The men would know how to get to our parents, as they have lived in the city before. "Where is Shok?" I ask, as Love did not mention him.

"Oh, he's outside, making sure no one finds us."

"So, I missed all the excitement," I quip as I stand, making sure my head doesn't dip again.

"Oh, you have no idea." At Love's laugh, I look at her. Something must have happened to amuse her like this. "You know those shorts that Trek wanted Hope to change out of?" I nod. "Well, looks like she is the only one dressed in a fashion that the humans won't suspect who we are." I smile, imagining Hope's comments when she found out that she was right after all.

"Did she give him hell?"

Love laughs. "Oh yes. When Shok mentioned the fact that she looked fine, the first thing she did was turn to Trek and raise her brows. Needless to say, Trek charged out of here, and Hope charged right after him." We both laugh just as Drez and Shok come in from a side door that I hadn't seen.

"Good, you are awake," Shok says with a smile, "and feeling well, I see."

"You need to eat," Drez mutters as he lifts two big bags onto the seat next to Love.

"Oh, what did you get? I'm starving," Shok mutters as he opens one of the bags.

"For you and Trek, I got burgers with fries. For the rest of us, vegetable curry." He has tied his hair up in a bun, a style I have never seen before but enhances his handsome features. He covered his ears with his hair, which I'm guessing here in the human world is prudent.

"How did you pay for it?" Shok asks as he lifts a box out of the bag. "Oh, man, I have missed these." He opens his box to show a bun filled with meat and garnish, and there is some red liquid dripping from it. It doesn't look very appetizing, but he seems to love it.

"Remember that trick Brog showed us with the ATMs? Well, it comes in handy when we need it," Drez says as he hands me a package. "Careful, it's hot."

Taking a bite, I gasp. I have never eaten something so spicy. My taste buds are tingling as I try to familiarize myself with the food, but in a strange way, I like it. "I hope you got us some of that," Hope says as they join us. Drez hands them their meals and then goes back to his food.

"Well, one thing good about this is that you brought us to where your parents are," Trek says as he opens his food. "I was thinking that after everyone changes into appropriate clothing, we head out to find them."

"You must see this place," Hope says as she looks at Love and me. "It has buildings everywhere, and cars. People hardly talk to each other, and there are hardly any animals." She grimaces at that. "The trees, they have them in areas called parks. Can you believe that?" She takes a bite of her food and then frowns, looking at it closely before taking another bite.

"Did you see anything that you like?" Love asks.

"Yes, the clothes," she murmurs. "Oh, Dream, did Love tell you that I am dressed appropriately for here?" At that, she raises a brow at Trek, who conveniently ignores her.

"Yes, she did," I murmur. "What did you get us to wear?" I ask, frowning, as I can just imagine her getting the two of us shorts like hers just to make a point.

"I got something they call jeans; I think you will like it and the T-shirts." I wonder what these jeans are, but whatever it is, I will have to use them until we reach our parents.

"Did you get me a hoodie?" Shok asks. With his pronounced features and size, it is clear that he isn't human, but I'm not sure a hoodie will fit his size.

"Yes, and let me tell you, it wasn't easy. You do know it's summer now, so hoodies are scarce, and if you go outside in one, they are going to think you are a criminal," Trek quips as he takes the last bite of his food.

Shok shrugs and grins. "Just because I'm perfect doesn't mean you have to hate," he teases. Trek raises a brow at him as he continues. "Remember who all the women were after last time we were here?"

"What? You mean the statues?" Trek teases, which has all of us laughing as Shok shrugs good-naturedly. Being a Gargoyle among other Fae isn't always easy, as most say that Gargoyles have hearts of stone, but I know the truth. Shok has the kindest heart, and it is definitely not made of stone.

"Did you like someone when you were here?" Love asks, a frown adorning her petite face.

"No, no, I'm just joking," Shok replies as he raises his hand to scratch his head. Love looks over at Trek to get his comments, but Trek simply shrugs in reply. I wonder if Drez liked anyone when he was here, but if he did, I don't want to know about it, because I will start obsessing, wondering what she looked like, how she was, and it will get me into a bad mood.

"I'm done. Where are my clothes and I will go change," Shok says, changing the subject, which has Hope inclining her head towards the bags that Trek placed on the ground when they arrived. He lifts one bag, then another before he finds the hoodie that Trek and Hope got for him. I see that there is also a T-shirt and a pair of dark-blue pants. "You found jeans that will fit me?" Shok asks as he looks at the pants that I now know is what they call jeans.

"Well, we hope it fits you," Hope says as she finishes her meal before turning to Shok. "Hand me the bag." Shok reaches towards it, but Trek beats him to it. Taking the bag, she starts to pull out items of clothing, distributing them to all of us. In the meantime, Shok leaves to go get dressed. I lift my T-shirt and jeans up to look at them and smile as I see that my T-shirt is black with a Witch on a broom in silver across the front.

"I see you chose the clothes," Love says as she starts to laugh as Trek lifts his T-shirt up and we see the words across it say *I'm a real dog.* I cannot hold it in when he turns it towards himself and reads the words. His frown is dark as he glares at Hope. As a Werewolf, being called a dog is the worst thing anyone can call them. Werewolves do not like to be placed in the same category as dogs.

"Very funny," he mutters as he also turns and follows in the direction Shok went.

"I guess I better also go get changed. You three can change in here and come out when you're done," Drez says as he follows the other two men.

"That was so mean," Love says, still smiling.

"He has been getting on my nerves the whole day. He deserved it," Hope mutters as she stands. "Shall we change? I'm curious to see how these jeans look."

"Where can we change? Anyone can look in here with all these windows," I say, only to have Love take hold of my hand and pull me behind her.

"It's really small in there, but it's private," Love says as she opens a door and shows me what must be a bathroom, but which is so small that anyone will have difficulty to move. "Apparently it's the toilets they have in the trains for anyone who might need them. Just leave the door open. When you're done, I will go in and change, and like that, it's private."

I change while Love stands at the door. Just as I finish, Hope walks up to the door, already wearing her jeans and a purple top. "What do you think?" she asks as she twirls around.

"Where did you get changed?" I ask, looking behind her to see if there is anywhere else she could have gone.

"In the other bathroom on the other side," she says. "So?"

"I think those jeans look really good on you, and the top fits your body perfectly," Love says. "You, too, Dream. I think if mine looks as good on me as they do on the two of you, then I have just found myself a new favourite."

I step out of the toilet, pleased to be out of that tight space. "I wonder if we will see Mom and Dad today?" I say. Not speaking to them on the phone every week like we used to has made me miss them. Even though they're not around often, we love them dearly and they love us. We know that everything they do is to keep us safe, and I know that if my father knows that something is threatening his daughters, he will move heaven and hell to keep us safe.

"I don't know. Trek seemed concerned with the fact that we hadn't seen any Fae while we were out. According to him, we should have at least seen one." I frown. Is it possible that the Fae here are in danger?

"How does it look?" Love asks as she steps out of the bathroom in her jeans and blue T-shirt. I smile at her as she twirls.

"Looks great," I say.

"Suits you, Love," Hope says, and then she takes my hand, squeezing it gently. "Whatever is going on in Eternity Fae, hopefully we will figure it out soon with Mom and Dad's help."

"I just think that if Dad knew about the shadows, he would have been there already fighting them. I'm worried that something might have happened to them." After broaching my concerns, I feel guilty in worrying them too.

"I'm sure they are fine, and they just don't know that anything is happening, or they might just be fighting whatever it is from out here," Hope says with a smile as she starts leading the way out of the train, our normal clothes in a bag so that we can carry it with us. Looking around, I see that there is nothing left behind to indicate that we might have been here.

Making our way outside, I see the three men on the other side to where we are, a serious look on their faces. "Well, hello there, you sexy ladies," Shok says, which has Drez glaring at him and Trek punching him in the arm. "What?"

“Thank you, Shok. It’s nice to feel appreciated,” Hope says, which has Trek frowning at her and Shok grinning as he tweaks his eyebrows at the other two men.

“Watch and learn,” he says.

“Enough. Let’s get going. We have decided to try one of the Fae shelters we know of that is close to here,” Drez says as he inclines his head for us to follow him.

“But I thought we were going to see our parents,” I state, only to have him stop and turn to look at me.

“We will, but with everything that has been happening, we thought it would be prudent to first find out what has been going on here before we go knocking on their door.” I frown, seeing the logic behind the plan but wishing that we could go to them instead. “Are you all ready?” he asks, looking around at everyone before once again turning to make his way up an embankment. “Dream, walk next to me.”

I frown. “I’m fine here,” I mutter, only to hear Love giggle. When I glance at her, I see her trying to hold a straight face. She’s clearly not trying too hard, because when I glare at her, she lets it slip and grins openly at me. Suddenly, I smack into something solid and would have fallen back down the embankment if strong arms didn't grab my upper arms. Squeaking in surprise, I look up to see Drez's face above mine.

"I wasn't asking you. We are not back in Eternity Fae. It is dangerous here with things you don't know anything about, and you can't use your magic here and our weapons are useless if someone pulls out a gun and shoots you. So, for me to be able to protect you, you will walk next to me." Drez isn't a man of many words, but when he does speak, he doesn't mince his words.

"Argh, okay," I mutter, which has him letting go of my arms and waiting until I start making my way up. The others are ahead of us, but I know they are all paying attention to what is being said here. "Don't think you will always get your way."

"I will get my way when it is necessary," he replies, not once glancing at me as we finally make it to the road. I see the cars zooming past. I have heard about them and seen pictures, but they don't make up for the real thing and the noise. I am about to step down from where we are walking, when Drez clamps his hand around my upper arm again.

"Are you trying to kill yourself?" he grunts just as a car zooms past where I would have been. The sudden appearance of the car has me freezing in shock. "Walk on this side." He guides me to his other side before we continue walking. After walking for a couple minutes, I notice that the men are taller than most of the men I have seen today, not just taller but better looking too.

I know that the humans don't know that we exist, and one law that all Fae need to abide to is not to share our identity with any human, as it is considered an offense with a high punishment, but when I look around, they seem so harmless. We have been walking for a couple hours when Trek stops across the road from a tall warehouse-looking building. I see him raise his head as he scents out the area, a frown on his face.

"Stay here, I will be right back," he says as he makes his way across the road.

"What's wrong?" Love asks as she looks up at Shok questioningly.

"He is just being careful; we can't just bring three princesses in there without staking out the place and who is inside first." I hate being called a princess, but at the end of the day, that is what we are. We wait for a couple minutes before Trek makes his way back to us.

"So?" Hope asks as soon as he reaches us.

"We have a problem." At his serious face, I feel my stomach tensing. We are in a new place completely alien to us, without knowing how to get back, and when we think we have found a way, it seems like obstacles keep appearing in our way. "It seems your parents have gone missing."

CHAPTER 11

"What?" Hope and Shok say simultaneously. "What do you mean our parents are missing?"

"Come, let's go inside and they will explain," Trek says as he inclines his head towards the building behind him. The six of us make our way inside to find about thirty people inside. Looking around, I can tell there are Elves, Werewolves, even two Vampires, which we don't see much of in Eternity Fae but I know exist here in the city.

"What kind of place is this?" I whisper to Drez.

"If Fae are finding difficulty integrating or have a problem, then we have some of these homes throughout the cities welcoming them among their own people so that we may help," Drez answers.

"Are there always this many?" I ask, only to have Drez shake his head.

"No, this is more than usual," he murmurs before we come to a standstill among them.

"I know you," one of the men in the group says as he points at Shok. "You are one of our sovereign's men."

"Where are they? What has happened to them? Why have they disappeared?" a woman asks loudly from the back.

"We don't know. We have only just gotten here," Trek says as he lifts his hands for quiet.

"How can you not know? He's one of the protectors," the same man says.

"We haven't been here. We have only just arrived in the city," Shok says, taking a step forward. "Why do you say that our sovereigns are missing?"

"Because there is a war brewing, and they are not doing anything about it. When there has been requests to meet with them, the requests are denied." My heart is racing at what they are saying. What if something happened to them? I know that my parents would never let anyone get hurt if it was within their power to stop it.

"They most probably went to Eternity Fae and are hiding there until everything is over," another man says from the left.

"How dare you? They would never hide. They have always been there for the Fae. If they are not now, that only means that something has happened," Hope says angrily. "Instead of complaining and inventing stories, have any of you actually tried to find out the truth?"

Most of the people before us lower their heads in embarrassment. Others scowl in anger at Hope's words. "Those who have been to see them say that they were told the queen and king are in Eternity Fae."

"That is a lie. We have just come from Eternity Fae, and they are not there," Love says angrily, which has most of them looking at each other in surprise.

"That's not possible," a woman says from my right. "We have tried to get to Eternity Fae, but it's closed a magic spell keeping everyone out, now who do you know that can do that except for the sovereign."

"Look, what she says is true. We have just come from Eternity Fae Forest, and the sovereigns are not there. That is why we came here, because there is something attacking everyone there, and we thought that maybe someone here in the city would know what it is." Everyone stands in shock at my revelation. "Why don't you tell us what exactly has been happening here so that we can try to figure out what is happening."

"A couple months back, Fae started disappearing. At first, we all thought it was a Fae hunter, but as time progressed and more went missing, we realized that no Fae hunter could outsmart so many Fae and come out unscathed, so the only solution was that it was another Fae doing this," a Grundel standing to the front says.

I am surprised to see a Grundel here, as Grundels are frequently found in the homes of Elves. Grundels work in service for the Elves in exchange for a safe and happy home. They are dedicated to Elves and their families and usually live together with them for generations, moving with them as necessity dictates. To see a Grundel here away from the Elves' home is surprising, unless his Elven family is here too.

"Was it a Fae?" Drez asks.

"We still don't know, but Fae are still disappearing, and now some have been found dead," someone states.

“How are they when they are found?” Drez asks.

“Like an animal attacked them, maybe a Werewolf,” one of the Vampires say, which clearly shows that the rift between the Vampires and Werewolves is still there.

“Are you blaming us for this?” a Werewolf who has been quiet until now asks, facing the Vampire. This is a volatile situation, and these Fae are nervous.

Trek moves forward to stand between where the Werewolf and Vampire are standing. “What is killing the Fae is not a Werewolf. The same thing is happening in Eternity Fae, and we have had the misfortune of meeting them. We call them shadows because that is what they are. We have found that the only way to beat the shadows is with light.” I can see the confused look on everyone’s face as Trek goes on to explain everything that has been happening at Eternity Fae and everything we have found out up to now. “So, by telling us everything you know about what has been happening here, we might be able to figure out who is behind this and who wants harm on the Fae.”

"Since the sovereign has disappeared, it has become worse. The Demons are out and about, attacking unhindered," one of the Vampires say. The Demons are Vampires who have overindulged when drinking from humans to the point of killing. When the Vampires get a taste for killing, they never go back, and then they must be killed, as they become dangerous to the human and Fae population. I have never faced a Demon, as we don't have them in Eternity Fae. The guards around Eternity Fae Forest keep them away.

"Drez, looks like you have your work cut out for you," Shok says as he looks over his shoulder at Drez, who is still standing next to me.

"You are Drez, the slayer of Demons?" the one Vampire asks in surprise, only to get a nod from Drez. I look up at him in surprise. He is called the slayer of Demons?

"Why do they call you the slayer of Demons?" I ask.

"They say that whatever Demon the slayer has targeted is a dead Demon. There is no other Fae who has killed as many Demons," the same Vampire says, still looking at Drez in fear.

"Good thing you are back," the Grundel says, a speculative look on his face. "If you need any help with anything, just let me know. I am free to serve you."

I smile as I see Drez frown. I don't think Drez is the type of Elf to have others do things for him, as he is very much a loner and does everything himself.

"I'll keep that in mind," he mutters.

"Do any of you know how to heal a Fae once they have been attacked by one of these shadows you are talking about?" a Fairy says from the back, and from where I am standing, I can see the concern on her face.

"If you let us see the Fae, we will be able to tell you if we are able to help or not," Love says as she starts making her way towards the Fairy, but is stopped by Shok as he steps before her.

"Where is the wounded?" he asks, not showing any sign when Love slaps his back in anger.

"At the back. Please, he isn't doing well. He was attacked yesterday." Shok looks over his shoulder at an angry Love and winks.

"Shall we go have a look?" Love glares at him as she walks past him, muttering to herself. I smile as Hope and I follow her, with Drez and Shok taking up the rear. I see that Trek stayed behind, and I'm guessing that is to try to get as much information from these Fae as possible. As we approach, I can see a male Fairy lying on a makeshift bed. His colouring is pale, and his breathing is laboured. His wings have been released from the holding that the Fairies usually use here in the city, and they are hanging down limp and colourless.

"Do you mind giving us some space to examine him?" Hope asks of the Fairy anxiously standing next to him. She nods, stepping back, which immediately has Hope pulling down the sheet covering him, only to groan at the raw, infected wounds across his stomach and arm. As I look at the wounds, it is clear that he was attacked by one of the shadows. We are going to have to try to get the word out that to stay safe, the Fae are to have as much light as they can always around them.

"He's very weak," Love says from next to me, her hand taking mine and squeezing. I know that she is trying to assure herself as much as me, because even though we have healed Brog and Braun before from an attack, they were not as weak as this male now is.

“Dream,” Hope calls from the other side of the Fairy, “I think you start by expelling all the darkness from his body. As soon as I see that most of the darkness has been expelled, I will fill him with energy and life to try to revive him and bring him back to health.” Hope then looks at Love. “Love, you can bring him peace and calmness once I am done.”

I move to kneel next to the bed, but before I can, Drez is pulling a chair behind me. “Sit,” he murmurs before moving back. Sitting down, I look up at Hope to see her looking at me. She smiles her encouragement and nods. Closing my eyes, I stretch out my hands and place them over his chest, flinching when I feel the heat of his body. This Fairy is burning up. As soon as I start flowing light into him, I feel as if a rush of fury crashes against my energy, and then I’m gasping for air as a hand around my neck squeezes the air out of me.

My eyes pop open as I struggle to breathe, seeing the Fairy’s eyes are now open and staring at me, the orbs a pitch black, as he squeezes.

"Let go of her or you will be the one struggling for breath," I hear Drez say just as his hands are taking hold of the Fairy's and pulling them away from my neck.

"Dream, oh," Love cries out as she pulls me from my chair, giving Shok and Drez space to subdue the possessed Fairy.

"Well, now we know what happens to the Fae who get attacked by the shadows," Hope says as she comes around to hug me. "Looks like they don't die; they just become evil."

"Who would go to such lengths to make the Fae evil?" Love asks as she strokes my hair as I slowly start regulating my breath.

"No, please don't hurt him," the Fairy who asked for our help calls out as she rushes towards where Shok is. Taking hold of his muscular arm, she tries to pull him away, which is laughable, as Shok is the biggest of all the men.

He looks over at her and glares. "He will hurt everyone if we don't detain him. Don't worry, we won't hurt him." He looks up and over my shoulder. "A little help here," he mutters.

Looking over my shoulder, I see Trek approach, and then he guides the Fairy back.

"We need to do this. Calm down," Trek says.

"I'm going to try to bring out the darkness in him from here." My voice is hoarse as I whisper my intentions.

"No," Drez states, but it's too late. I think of the light extracting all the darkness out of him. The Fairy starts to scream in anger, thrashing around, which tells me that the light is affecting him, but I don't think it will help, as I don't think he has any goodness in him anymore. I can feel myself tiring at the strength of the evil combating my magic, until finally, I give up or it will drain me completely.

"I can't. I can't find any goodness in him anymore," I whisper, only to see Drez glaring at my clear disregard for his order.

"She called you Dream, and you Love. There are only two fairies I know who are called Dream and Love, and they are the sovereigns' daughters. Am I wrong?" I glance over at a Gargoyle standing against one of the pillars, looking at everything that is happening. Trek is suddenly beside the three of us, as Drez and

Shok are still subduing a violent Fairy, a frown on his face as he looks at everyone who is now looking at us suspiciously.

The men clearly didn't want anyone to know who we were because of everything that is going on and not being sure of how the Fae would react, but now it's too late, as realization is dawning on everyone's faces.

"What if they are?" Trek asks with a growl, which has the Gargoyle lifting his arms in the air in a submissive manner.

"Just curious why three princesses—because I am guessing she is also one of them," the Gargoyle says as he points to Hope, "would be coming here instead of going to see their parents." Everyone has gone deathly quiet at the interaction.

"As we said when we arrived, we were being attacked by the shadows at Eternity Fae. After one such attack, we were transported here into the city. We were hoping to ask for the help of the sovereign, as we have not had any communication from the outside in some time and didn't know what was happening here," Trek states as he looks at everyone.

"How did you transport here from Eternity Fae?" another Gargoyle asks as he steps closer.

"One of the princesses."

"That means she can transport us back to Eternity Fae," a Fairy says from the back.

"No, that does not mean that. A great deal of energy from all of us was required to be able to transport us here, and just because we were all about to be killed." At his revelation, the Fae present all start to comment, some angry that we will not try to transport them back to Eternity Fae, others just despondent at the situation. I feel a presence behind me. Turning my head, I see Drez has come to stand at my back, his expression angry. He places his hands on my upper arms, squeezing gently in comfort.

"Can you not see that we are at war? We need to stick together and fight this enemy who has decided to attack us. Fae are being killed and turned evil. Just look behind me. Do you want to end up like him or killed? Stop fighting each other and start trying to figure out what is actually happening and find solutions," Drez states forcibly. I have always admired the way he is so calm and collected and knows just what to say at the right time. I know I should not, but

I am so tired of this constant fight lately that all I want is a respite of everything.

Leaning back against his chest, I feel the warmth of his body against my back, giving me a feeling of safety. I feel him tense behind me, but then he relaxes, and his arm comes around my waist, holding me close. I have a feeling this war is here to stay, and I am going to need all the strength I can get.

CHAPTER 12

After a turbulent night where most of the Fae at the safe house had questions and many heated arguments were raised and then peace was forcefully installed by the men, we finally managed to make it through the night and are now on our way to where my parents are supposed to have been residing the last time anyone saw them.

"So, tell me about that moment I saw you and Drez having?" Love comes to sit next to Hope and me. After walking for half the day, the men guided us to this quiet park with tall oak trees and beautiful pathways that in a way give us peace and energize our souls by being surrounded by nature and not concrete, which the city is mostly surrounded by. Shok and Drez have gone out to get us something to eat. Trek leans against a tree, his eyes closed as he rests, but I can tell that he's not sleeping.

"What do you mean? What moment?" I ask innocently, which has Hope elbowing me.

“Come on, even I saw it,” Hope says with a grin.

“It was nothing. You saw how everyone was arguing, and I had just been strangled. He was just giving me some emotional support.” Love raises her eyebrows at me with an unbelieving expression on her face.

“Argh,” Hope mutters. “He likes you. It’s clear to see, and you are mad about him. Just accept it already.”

“He told me that protecting me was his job. You’re mistaken. He just wants to make sure that I am not harmed on his watch.”

“You’re so blind,” Love mutters as she shakes her head. “I will show you.”

“Love, don’t you dare mingle in this,” I state as I frown at her. “Are you somehow making him act as if he cares about me? I know you can enhance people’s feelings to make them realize when they care for someone.”

Love shakes her head emphatically. “No, of course not, but that isn’t a bad idea,” she teases, which has me lightly pushing at her shoulder.

“Don’t you dare.”

She raises her hands in surrender. "Fine, I'll let you two fools fumble around until you finally come to terms with what you both feel," she quips as she shrugs her shoulders. "And you, Hope, don't think I haven't noticed that you complain too much when a certain person is around."

I see Hope's look of surprise as she stares at Love, and then she shrugs. "Think what you will," she mutters just as Shok and Drez approach with a bag.

"Anyone hungry?" Shok asks with a wink that is mostly covered by the hoodie covering his face.

"I'm starving. I could eat a whole forest," I state as I smile at him.

"Well, I'm afraid we forgot about you," he states with an innocent look.

"Guess I'll just have to eat your lunch," I tease, which has him grinning.

"You eat meat? Sure, I would like to see that."

I had forgotten that he usually eats meat. Yuck, I can't stomach the thought of eating animals, and also because our metabolism isn't structured to eat something that needs so much digesting.

"Shok, if you didn't get me food, I would shave all that hair that you're so proud of off when you're sleeping," I threaten playfully, which has him grinning as he raises a hand before him as if warding me off.

"It's not my fault. Blame Drez. He ate yours on the way. Shave his hair," he says teasingly. "I dare you." I look over at Drez to see him shaking his head at our silliness. When he sees my eyes on him, he raises a brow in question as if daring me to try.

"I can't. He sleeps with one eye open," I quip.

"How would you know that? Have you been staring at him while he sleeps?" Love asks innocently, which has my cheeks flushing with colour.

"I thought everyone was hungry?" Drez asks, which saves me from this embarrassing moment as everyone turns their attention to the food he is handing out in separate containers.

"Do you think they are going to be there?" Love suddenly asks. She does not need to say who she is talking about, as we all know she's talking about our parents. To be honest, after everything I have heard, I worry that they have been taken, or worse, killed. I feel my stomach tightening at the thought that something might have happened to them.

"We don't know yet what is going on, but one thing I know about the sovereigns is that they don't get taken down easily. I know for a fact that they didn't run away like they were saying when we arrived, but that something has happened. That is obvious, or they would be fighting this evil that has befallen us for all to see," Trek says before taking a bite of his food.

"Maybe if we hadn't come here, we would have destroyed the source of sound and all the shadows would have vanished," I state, feeling angry at myself for having transported us here even if at the time I did not know what I was doing.

Love places her hand over mine and squeezes gently. "If you had not brought us here, we would all have died. We all know that those things were winning. I don't know what they were, but what I know is we are not prepared to fight them."

"They are stronger than the shadows, and light does not affect them," Shok mutters.

"Well, we used everyone's energy on them, and all it did was slow them down," Hope says as she steals a chip from Trek, which surprises me because Werewolves don't share their food with anyone except their mates.

"Well, we won't find anything out by sitting here. We better start making our way there," Drez says as he places his empty container in the bag.

"Is it still far from here?" I ask as I do the same. Picking up the bag, I start collecting everyone's empty containers and placing them in the bag.

"Maybe another hour or so and we will be there," Drez replies as I start making my way towards a bin that is just down the incline from where we are sitting. I hear the others talking as I stuff the bag into the bin, tensing when I hear footsteps approaching from my right.

"Well, hello there, beautiful," a man says as he walks past. Glancing at him, I see that he is walking a beautiful dog that reminds me of Beast but in a much smaller version. I know that Love is missing Beast, as she has not stopped talking about him and how he must be worried that she is not back. The dog barks, hurrying towards me. "Guess Thor thinks you're beautiful too," the man says with a laugh as I stretch out my hand to scratch the dog's head.

"Hello, Thor," I say as the dog lowers his head, happy to be getting attention. "My sister would love your dog; she has one just like him but much bigger."

"Is there a problem here?" I hear Drez grunt as he comes to stand next to me. I see the man tense, a surprised look on his face as he sees Drez.

"No, I'm just meeting Th—"

"Ohh," Love interrupts as she comes rushing towards me. "You're such a beautiful baby, aren't you?" she says as she falls on her knees before the dog, who immediately forgets all about me and starts to lick Love's hand.

"This is the sister I was telling you about," I say to the man, who is looking at his dog happily lapping at Love. "His name is Thor," I tell Love unnecessarily, because she is so entranced with Thor that she more than likely didn't even hear me.

"Come on, Love, we should be going," Shok says. Placing his hands on Love's waist, he starts to help her up, when Thor starts growling at him.

"Thor," the man calls, but to no avail. Looks like the dog does not like the attention being taken off him. "I don't know what has come over him. He is usually quite good." Love leans down and talks softly in the dog's ear, which immediately has him quieting.

"He's fine. He just loves the attention," she says to the man. "You are a good owner. Thor loves you." The man raises his eyebrows and smiles at her statement.

"Well, it was nice meeting you. We need to go," Trek says as he places his hand behind Hope's back, guiding her around the man.

"Bye," I call as I follow them with Drez walking beside me.

"Don't you think he looked like Beast? But my baby is unique. There is no other animal like him," Love says in a choked voice. "I wonder how he is doing."

"He will be fine. We will see him soon," I hear Shok say. Looking over my shoulder, I see Shok place his arm around Love's shoulders in a comforting hug. Smiling, I am turning my head forward, when I stumble and would fall if it weren't for Drez's quick reflexes. His arm comes across my waist, holding me up, flexing as he pulls me upright.

"Look where you are going," he mutters.

"Thank you," I answer, feeling embarrassed of how clumsy I seem; this is the second time he has had to save me from falling over. We continue making our way in silence, the scenery changing the closer we get to my parents'. High trees shade the streets. The houses are bigger and further apart, with big beautiful gardens that can be seen sometimes from the main gate. Flowers are in abundance on flower beds along the road. I hear Hope's sighs of pleasure every time she sees a new flower that she hasn't seen before.

"If we keep stopping to smell the flowers every time you see a new one, we will never get there," Trek mutters when she once again stops next to this beautiful bush filled with purple flowers.

Hope looks up at him and glares. "If you don't want to wait, then carry on. No one is stopping you," she says, lifting her head in rebellion.

"Stop being so rebellious," he mutters.

"Stop being so bossy," she responds.

"Okay, okay," Love intervenes as she comes to stand next to Hope. "We need to get to the house soon, Hope. It's starting to get dark." Hope sighs, but then she nods and continues making her way down the road. I smile at Trek as I see him shaking his head. I'm sure if no one was around, he would most probably roll his eyes too. At the thought of seeing Trek rolling his eyes, I grin; that is, until Shok stops before two houses down the road.

“Are you saying that you were kicking up a fuss, and meanwhile, we were nearly here?” Hope asks in disbelief as she looks over her shoulder at Trek, but he doesn’t reply as he looks around and then lifts his head, sniffing at the air.

“Can you smell that?” Hope says.

“What?” Shok asks, looking around cautiously.

“My frustration with him,” she says as she glares as Trek, who completely ignores her.

“Something is wrong,” he states.

“You don’t say. Have you only figured that out now?” Hope mutters sarcastically.

“One of these days, I’m going to spank the sass right out of you,” he mutters, glaring at her.

“Really, you and what army?” she asks sweetly.

“I don’t need anyone to help me with a surly child,” he shoots back, which has her placing her hands on her hips and glaring at him.

“Are we going to just stand here the whole day, shooting meaningless words at each other, or are we actually going to try to find out what is going on?" Drez grunts in annoyance, which has Trek lifting his hands in apology. "You were saying that something seems wrong. What can you smell?"

"Well, that is the problem. I can't scent anything. It's like there is no one inside."

I frown. How can there be no one inside? Even if my parents are not in residence, at least the guards would be around.

"Let's try the tunnels," Shok murmurs. "If anyone is inside, they won't know about the tunnels unless they're the sovereigns or one of the higher guards." I look at Shok in surprise. I never knew that my parents had tunnels here.

"We should have our weapons here," Love says as she looks inside and at the empty driveway, again suspicious because I would think that there would be guards at the entrance.

"When we get near the entrance to the tunnel, we can take them. For now, there are still humans who might see us and then call the police, which we don't want," Trek mutters as he starts making his way further down the road. My parents have a huge property, as is expected. Just before we get to the end of the wall to their property, Trek veers and walks behind a clump of bushes that are high and hide the wall. Following him, I am surprised to see him place his hand on the brick wall. I can tell that he is trying to sense if there is anyone on the other side, or scent if there are any strange smells.

"Let's be careful in there. We don't know what we might find in the tunnel," Drez states as he hands me my bow that he pulls out of the haversack that Trek acquired when looking for clothes when we arrived. He hands everyone their weapons, which we ready, before Trek moves a brick from the wall, and I see that there is some kind of beaker inside.

Looking around at us, he states, "The only way to open the protections to the tunnel is with a drop of royal blood." I look over at Hope, seeing the surprise on her face, which must be what mine is displaying as well.

"Here," Love mutters as she stretches out her hand towards Trek. I see him frown as he looks down at her hand and then back at her as he shakes his head. "Sorry, Love, but you will have to prick your own finger. We have promised an oath to never draw blood from any of you."

She sighs as she lifts her hand, and with one of her blades, she draws blood. Trek lifts her hand, pulling it into the opening on the wall so that the blood can drop into the beaker.

The minute the blood enters the beaker, I hear a grating sound, and then a piece of the wall slides back. “Dream, we might need light,” Shok mutters as we look into a tunnel encased in darkness. Stepping forward, I am about to step inside, when Drez stops me with a hand to my upper arm. He lifts his sword, his eyes transforming into the hypnotic blue, his sword lighting up too.

“Follow me,” he states. I lift my bow in readiness and feel myself shining light through my hands onto the bow and arrow. Immediately, the tunnel lights up, showing us debris scattered around the ground. It looks like no one has been in these tunnels in years, which in a way is a good thing. We walk for a distance before Drez stops, his body tensing. Trek squeezes past me until he is standing just behind Drez.

“I can scent Fae,” he mutters as he inclines his head slightly as if hearing for any noise that we cannot.

“I’m going ahead. Stay here,” Drez states as he starts making his way through the tunnel in a silent way that only the Elven can, as if a wisp of air moving through the tunnel. We must be standing here for about fifteen minutes, my stomach knotting more and more with each passing minute, when suddenly, I see him emerging from the darkness, his sword raised but unlit, as it's evident he was trying to not bring any attention to himself.

"What did you find?" Hope asks as he approaches.

"Three dungeons are filled with our people, but I don't see the sovereigns," he whispers.

"How many guarding them?" Shok asks.

Drez shrugs, a frown on his face. "I can't see anyone, but I know they are there. I saw a shadow for a split second before it was gone."

"That means that when we open the tunnel door, we have to be prepared to attack; they won't know we are coming, but we don't know how many we are up against," Trek states as he passes his fingers through his long hair.

"You three should stay in the tunnel just in case we don't make it," Drez states as he looks at me.

"That's not happening. We have been in this fight before with the three of you. I am coming," I state.

"So am I," Hope mutters from behind me.

"Same for me," Love joins in. I can see the displeasure on Drez's face, but that is just too bad, as I am not going to stay behind like a delicate flower while they go out there into danger to save all the captured Fae.

"Fine, but stay behind us," Shok states, which has Love looking up at him and huffing.

"If anyone stands behind you, they can't see anything happening in front," she states.

"Yes, and no one can see what is behind me either," he snaps, frowning at her.

"Don't use that tone with me, Shok," she says angrily.

"Then don't question me when I am trying to protect you," he states.

"Can you have this argument later?" I ask with a raised brow, which has both huffing in annoyance.

"Let's go," Drez says as he turns. "Dream, no light now, but we need as much light as possible when we open the door. I will let you know."

"Okay."

We make our way slowly through the darkness until we come to a dead end, which I am guessing is the door. Drez moves over for Trek to squeeze past. I see Trek looking through what seems like a chipped brick, but obviously is an opening for whoever is in the tunnel to look at the other area. Trek raises his head, scenting his surroundings.

"I would say at least seven," he whispers.

"Ready?" Drez asks in a whisper. As everyone nods, he looks at me. "Light." I immediately light up my bow and arrow, making it shine like a beacon as the tunnel door snaps back, and then chaos rains.

CHAPTER 13

I see a shadow screeching as it tries to move away from the light. I shoot the arrow that penetrates through it, making the shadow explode into little particles of light. Pulling out another arrow from behind me, I slot it into the bow and then move closer towards the darkness. Seeing a shadow move, I let the arrow fly, and another shadow disintegrates into little light particles, falling to the ground.

Drez cuts down shadows as he moves closer to the darkness, the light in his sword bright enough to have them disintegrate. I hear the others opening at the cell doors, analysing all the Fae inside as we go after the shadows. I am behind and to the left of Drez, following him as he penetrates more of the darkness, when a shadow rushes straight for me.

I jump in fright at the sudden appearance of it, letting the arrow fly spontaneously. It hits the shadow just as it's about to reach me. There seems to be more shadows than we thought, because I am sure that Drez has dispelled at least five shadows. With my three, it is at least eight, and I sense that there are more in the darkness.

Moving closer to Drez, I touch his back, which immediately has the sword lighting up the whole dungeon with its brightness. We see two shadows that were lying in wait on the side-lines quickly trying to retreat, but I let go of Drez and shoot an arrow at the one on my side while Drez rushes towards the other, cutting him down before he can leave.

"Are there any wounded among you?" Hope asks as she stands near one of the dungeon doors.

"Not in here," comes from one of the cells.

"Two in here, but we have restrained them," comes from another cell, but there is no answer from the third cell. Walking closer to the door, I shine light inside to about ten Fae tied and gagged. One of them seems wounded.

"Why are these restrained and none of you are restrained in your cells?" I ask, looking over my shoulder to the faces of the dirty and scared Fae in the other cells.

"They are the sovereigns' guards," one says.

"Where is the king and queen?" Love asks.

"When we were ushered in here, the fighting was still going on above," someone says from the cell where there are no wounded. “Most of us are from the kitchen or cleaning staff.”

“I think only the guards might know where they are,” another says from the other cell. “Let us out.”

“Not yet. We need to make sure that all the shadows have gone before we let you go, or the same thing will happen, or worse.”

“It wasn’t the shadows who attacked,” one man says from the back of one of the cells.

“Then who?” Trek asks.

“They wore capes. I couldn’t see their faces. For a split second, it looked like they didn’t have one, but that doesn’t make sense,” a female troll states. I look over at Hope to see her grimace. That can only be the creatures we encountered when we were near the source of the sound. If it’s true and those things are above, then we are in more trouble than I thought, because if we did not conquer them last time, I don’t see a way that we are going to conquer them now. I hear a crack. Glancing over, I see that Shok has broken the lock on the door of the guards’ cell. He walks in and stops. “Hello, boys, bet you didn’t expect to see me.” I hear grunts.

"I'm going to take this out of your mouth, but if you kiss me, I'm putting it right back." I smile at how he still finds the will to tease in the eyes of what we are going through. He gently pulls the gag out of the one guard's mouth.

"How long have you all been down here?" Trek asks from the front of the one cell.

"It feels like forever," one says, "but I'm sure it has been a couple days. They have not given us anything to eat, but we have been given water eight times, which leads me to believe that we have been down hear for just over a week if they were giving us water once a day." They must be famished; I wish I could give them some food, but we didn't carry any with us.

Hope kneels on the ground, and I see her moving her hands around, which lets me believe that she must be trying to feel the energy of the earth below us. "Move away from the centre of the cell," she states before closing her eyes. I see everyone inside the two cells look at each other as they slowly move towards the sides of the cells just as the floor starts to crack and raise. The Fae in the cells gasp as buds start to spring out of the ground and then grow. I smile as I see Hope doing what she does best—make things grow.

In a couple minutes, there is an apple tree in each cell. The Fae are all looking at Hope open mouthed. As Fairies, we naturally have the gift of nurturing and growing flowers and trees, but not to Hope's extent. "Well, don't stand there looking at me. I thought you would be hungry." At that, they remember the apples and hurry to the tree, taking one each to eat. I know that the Gargoyles and Werewolves do not eat much fruit or vegetables, but they will have to adjust for a little while until it is safe to get them out.

"Where are the sovereigns?" I hear Shok asking. Glancing behind me into the cell where Shok is, I see the guard whisper something.

"Are you sure?" he asks, and I see the guard nod. Drez is untying the other guards and taking off their gags. It is evident that these men all know each other by the way they interact. "Hope, can you do your thing in here, too, please?" Shok asks.

"You brought them to a war? They will not be pleased," one of the men states in a rough dry voice as he inclines his head towards me.

"They are safer here than in Eternity Fae," Drez states. "Now get your strength back. Eat some apples." At that, some of the men groan. "Because this war is just starting,"

"I will try to bring you something else to eat if there is anything above," Trek says, but most of the men immediately start shaking their heads and grunting.

"The food was dosed. It made us weak," one man states, and then immediately starts coughing. I look over my shoulder at the cell that holds most of the kitchen staff. Does that mean that one of the Fae in that cell is a traitor?

This just assures us that we can't let anyone loose until we are sure of what is going on. I see the man Shok was talking to take hold of his hoodie and pull him closer before he whispers something else to him, which has Shok nodding before he rises. "We will be back as soon as we can." I retreat outside the cell at Shok's words, waiting until Drez and him are outside and the door is once again secure. Because Shok broke the lock to get in, Drez now had to jam a piece of metal to keep the door locked. I see that Love has been busy lighting all the torches, which will hopefully keep any shadows away.

"Let's go," Trek says as he stands by the door. Drez once again takes the lead, his sword at the ready, guiding the way up the stairs. At the door, he stops. Opening it a crack, he looks outside before closing it again.

"I cannot see anyone, but it's dark outside, which means there must be more of those shadows and maybe creatures out there. If we were alone, I might risk it, but I think in our situation, it is better if we wait until morning." I would complain, but to be honest, I am exhausted, and if we are going out there, I would rather do it in the daylight so that we have more of a chance.

"Does that mean we have to wait here?" Love asks as she looks around the stairs, which are narrow and made of stone.

"No, come," Shok murmurs as he turns. Walking down a couple stairs, he suddenly turns into a little crevice in the wall. Only when I approach do I see that it's a tight entrance that has been cleverly concealed with rock. Following Love into this opening, I see Shok hunching his shoulders and head to enter through a doorway that has been cut out from the rock. When I walk in, I am surprised to see an area furnished with four chairs and a single bed against the one wall. The room is small but big enough for the six of us.

"I will take the first watch just in case someone comes up or down the stairs," Trek says as he looks around the enclosure.

"Don't worry about that. I can close the entrance with vines. No one will find us in here," Hope says as she looks over her shoulder at Trek.

"Well, who said it wasn't good to have gifted fairies around?" Shok quips as he grins at Hope.

"Careful, or I will tie you up with the vines too," Hope teases as she walks to the door, stopping when she encounters Trek in her way. "You need to get out of the way for me to do this." Trek steps inside, but I can see that he doesn't relish the fact of being in here. Does he have an issue with confined spaces? I don't ask, but I keep an eye on him.

Shok lights a little oil lamp in the corner that allows for just enough light in the enclosure for us to see each other. Hope kneels at the entrance, placing her hands on the ground, focusing. A couple minutes later, there are vines growing up to the top, completely closing off this area.

"I'm hungry," Love says as she takes a seat on one of the chairs. "Maybe I'll just go to sleep so I can forget about it." I can see her disgruntled features in the dim light. Shok walks up behind Love's chair and strokes her head gently.

"Maybe Hope can whip something up," Shok says as Hope approaches.

"What can I whip up?" she asks as she comes to stand before Love's chair.

"Shok was thinking that maybe you could get us something to eat like you did with the apples," I reply, and she frowns.

"What do you think I am, mother nature?" she asks as she looks around at us. "You do know we aren't on the ground, as we have been upstairs, and the only reason I was able to get the vines is because vines grow through any crack."

"It's okay, Hope. We can wait for tomorrow," Love says with a gentle smile.

"I have something that I bought for Dream, but there are enough for the three of you. It's nothing that will fill you up, but it might put a smile on your faces," Drez says, which has me glancing over at him to see him pulling something out of his pocket. And then he holds them up. There are three lollipops just like the ones I love eating.

"Oh, you got those for me?" I am so pleased with the lollipop that I place my arms around his waist and hug him. I feel him tense, but just as I am about to pull away, his arms come around me and he is hugging me back. When I pull away, I look up at him to see him smiling. "Thank you. I haven't had one of these in a while."

"I know," he murmurs, handing me one. He then hands Hope and Love the others.

"Thank you," Love and Hope murmur. I see Trek looking around, and then he walks towards one of the chairs and takes a seat.

"What did you learn from the guards?" he asks, looking at Shok.

"They think that there is an infiltrator in the kitchen." I was right in my assumptions. "They say that the sovereigns were taken and thrown in the pit, but only after they were tied and a chain with a stone was placed around their necks."

"Does that mean they are alive?" I ask.

"Of course they are alive," Hope mutters as she takes the chair next to Trek as she opens the lollipop before popping it into her mouth.

"Yes, they were alive when they were thrown in the pit, but the sovereign king was injured." At Shok's statement, I feel my heart lurch in fear. Oh no, if he was injured by one of the shadows, he might be evil by now. The thought of my father being anything but the caring, joking father that he is is unbearable. My parents, even though different, are mates, which means if one dies, the other will soon follow, as they will have no will to continue.

"How badly?" Love asks, looking at Shok as he takes the last chair next to her.

"I don't know."

"Maybe we should take a chance and just try to make it to them tonight," I say, only to hear the men disagree immediately.

"If the sovereign king is wounded, we wouldn't be able to help him in his condition if we're fighting whatever is out there too," Drez states as he takes a seat on the mattress. "Come sit down, Dream. You must be tired."

I know he is right, and if we did get attacked while trying to rescue my parents when injured, it might get them and ourselves killed. Approaching the mattress, I take a seat next to Drez.

"The best thing to do is to try to get some rest, and when we wake up, we go," Trek states. Drez inclines his head behind him.

"Sleep. You will feel better when you wake up," he murmurs to me.

"What about you?" I ask. The mattress is small and will only fit one person. Even with my small stature, we won't fit two of us on here.

He slides off the bed until his back is against the mattress, his head leaning back against it. "I will be fine" I feel guilty for taking the only mattress in the room, but when I look at the others, I see Trek has sat on the floor with his back against the wall, his legs stretched out. Hope has stretched out next to him, her head on his lap. Those two are like cats and dogs, but then you see them like that.

Looking over at Shok, I see him placing the four chairs next to each other. Then he inclines his head towards them for Love to lie down. Once she has stretched out carefully on them, he sits down on the ground, his back against the chairs, his head back, leaning against Love's side. I sigh and then stretch out on the mattress and close my eyes. Tomorrow is not written yet. All we have is now and the hope that everything will go well.

CHAPTER 14

"Stay behind me," Drez whispers as we reach the door that leads outside. After a very restless night, we all woke up ready to leave the enclosure as soon as possible. It was stuffy and cramped with all of us in there. I pull an arrow from the pouch on my back. The sun is just coming up, which means that there shouldn't be any shadows outside, but with everything I have seen lately, I wouldn't be surprised if they turned up.

Trek opens the door. Looking around, he steps out. Shok follows, and then Drez. I follow, taking in a deep breath of the fresh air. It's not the clean air of Eternity Fae Forest, but it's better than the musty air of the enclosure where we spent our night.

Trek steps to his left, taking a few steps away from Shok, who is in the middle, and then Drez also moves a couple steps away from Shok to his right in a V formation. The three of us follow their actions, our weapons ready as we walk forward. I look around, seeing what must have been a beautiful garden, as it would be nothing else with my mother around. Now flowers are shrivelled, and dying trees are looking sick and withered.

"Look," Hope says, pointing up at the turrets on the roof of the mansion. Looking up, I frown. There are four grotesques on the turrets looking out at the whole property. They don't seem to be damaged, which means that there is no reason they wouldn't be in the dungeons with the other Fae. Something isn't right. As guards, they would have changed and been down here in their Gargoyle states by now.

"Something isn't right," Shok states as he also looks up. "One of the grotesques is Sham." I frown as I try to place which one is Shok's younger brother, but from this great distance, I can't tell which one it is. I see Shok start making his way towards the mansion, but Trek stops him with a hand to his shoulder.

"Let's find the sovereigns first before we venture into the mansion." I see Shok's resistance, and I understand that he wants to see why his brother isn't making his way down here too, but as the head of the guard, his priority is to the king and queen. He nods and then shrugs Trek's hand off his shoulder as he makes his way towards the side of the mansion.

We all continue, warily looking around as I am sure we can all feel that something is not right. The energy around the mansion feels heavy and oppressed. I can see the appeal that my parents have in living here. I am sure that at another time, it was beautiful and peaceful and nothing like the city we have travelled. The closer we get to the side, I start to hear a noise. "Oh no, do you hear what I am hearing?" The same sound that we heard before is here, but not as strong as in Eternity Fae Forest. I'm sure with time, it will increase in sound, but for now, it's still bearable.

"Love, this time, instead of me using all the energy to combat the sound, why don't you try using the sound of your words and drawing all our energy to combat it? Sound against sound."

She nods. "I'm not sure I know how to draw all the energy to me so that I can expel it through my voice, but I will try."

"There is something moving behind those trees," Drez warns, looking towards a cropping of trees on the far side of the property. "Not enough darkness there to be the shadows."

"Where is the pit?" Hope asks as she looks towards the cropping of trees.

"At the edge of those trees," Trek mutters as he pulls his blades out of their holsters, the long blades shining in the sunrise. As we approach, the sound gets louder and louder, which makes Love start singing. I can feel the vibrations cascading through my body, making it feel heavier, denser. I draw closer to Love and feel my energy connecting with hers, which amazes me, as she's not touching me but somehow is drawing it from me.

Hope follows my lead, and I see her raise her brows as she, too, feels the pull of her energy. "You go, Love. Suck us dry," she quips.

"Talk for yourself," I tease just as we hear a screeching sound, and then one of those hooded creatures that attacked us in Eternity Fae comes charging out of the forest towards us. "Oh no, not them again," I mutter as I light up my arrow and aim it towards the creature. Love's words are flowing through me, blocking out the vibrations that I was feeling before. I am feeling lighter and at peace.

"You all continue. I will fight him," Trek states, and then he rushes towards the creature.

"We're supposed to do this together. What doesn't he understand about teamwork?" Hope mutters angrily.

"Let's hurry up," Shok says as he starts jogging closer towards the clump of trees. We take off after him, Drez just behind him, and then the three of us. As soon as we enter the cropping of trees even though not in shadows and quite a lot of light coming through, there is an eerie feeling, which is understandable, as we see what looks like a web above where the pit is, and in the centre of the web above the pit is a red sphere rotating, making the sound that we can hear.

Love sings louder. The sphere seems to lose some of its speed but doesn't stop. The web shines a dazzling burgundy colour that speaks to evil forces. Whoever is doing this has powerful magic, and I'm not sure we are up to its power.

Raising my bow, I aim at the web. Filling the arrow with light, I imagine it sizzling through the arrow. "Love, I will shoot my arrow at the centre. You do your thing when I shoot it. Hope, do you want to draw light from me and shine it through the vegetation into the area in the sphere?"

Hope comes to stand near me. Kneeling, she places her hand on the ground and the other on my leg. I hear a commotion and know that Shok and Drez will hold back anything trying to stop us. “To save Mom and Dad,” Hope states as she closes her eyes.

“To save Mom and Dad,” I state, building the light in my mind to a point where it is blinding.

“To save Mom and Dad,” Love states.

“Now,” Hope orders. I shoot the arrow, seeing a flash of light as blinding as the sun following the arrow to penetrate the web and hit the sphere. Love is singing the word Love in a high, haunting voice that I have never heard before but that has my whole body tingling. I can feel every fibre in my body rushing through me. Feel the ground moving under me as I see the ground rising and falling as Hope sends energy through the ground to light up the area inside the web.

When the arrow penetrates the web, I see what looks like cracks appear throughout it. The burgundy starts to lighten. The light radiates out and up through every crack until the web starts to shatter. The sphere slows, the colour dulling the sound, diminishing until it finally stops. The brightness on the ground inside the sphere lights up, every blade of grass alight with a radiant green. Then the light that was shining starts glowing a light pink that begins rotating around the whole web in an anticlockwise motion, making it seem like the energy is undoing whatever magic was done before. The pink glow is from Love's energy that has amalgamated with mine and Hope's.

There is a loud screech from behind us as the creatures lose their source of energy, and then a loud shattering sound as the web disintegrates and the sphere disappears. We all stop casting our magic, and an eerie quiet fills the area around us. I feel drained, as if every part of me has been beaten, but to know that we managed to win this battle has me smiling.

I make my way towards where the sphere was and stop. The Pit has an iron cast covering that will need the strength of the men, because the way I feel, I won't be able to pick up anything heavier than a flower. "Is anyone in there?" Hope calls as she leans over the covering.

I hear footsteps behind me. Turning, I see the three men approaching. All three look worse for wear. Their clothes are torn, and their hair has come loose from the man buns they had been wearing, but I don't see any wounds. "No one is answering," Hope says. "Maybe the covering is containing the sounds."

Shok leans down next to Hope and tries to lift the lid, but it doesn't move. "Some help here," he mutters, which has Trek and Drez joining him. “Okay, on three,” he mutters as he places both his hands against the covering, the other two doing the same. “One, two, three.” On three, they put all their strength into moving the covering, but it doesn’t budge.

“What the hell?” Trek mutters.

“There most probably is a magic spell on the covering too,” Love says as she crosses her legs and sits on the ground. “To be honest, I don’t think I have any energy left.” I can see her disappointment; it portrays the rest of ours. Once the web disintegrated and the sphere stopped, we thought we could just get to our parents, but it seems like whoever did this had other plans.

“You three have used up all your energy, but we still have ours. It’s time to use it,” Trek says as he looks at the other two men. Shok grunts his agreement and Drez nods. A minute later, Drez’s eyes are a magnetic blue, which means that his powers are flowing through his body. Shok rotates his shoulders as his body starts to harden, and he starts changing into his grotesque self, harder, stronger, and bigger.

Trek’s body starts to widen, and fur starts to sprout around his body, but he doesn’t change fully and only enough to get his wolf’s strength.

They once again lean down, take hold of the covering, and a few seconds later, I see the covering moving. It still seems heavy, as all three men's muscles are straining, but it moves. Only halfway but enough.

They let it drop as they take in deep gulping breaths to recuperate their strength. "Is there anyone down there?" I ask as I lean over the opening, encountering only darkness.

"Mom, Dad, are you in there?" Hope calls. We all wait in silence, but there is no response. "Do you think they can't hear us? Or maybe they have taken them somewhere else." I close my eyes, trying to muster as much light as I can. Instead of the radiant bright light I usually materialize, a dull beam shines down into the pit.

"Can you see anything?" I ask as Hope and Love also lean over to look inside.

"No, it's too dark," Love mutters, but just then, a blue beam joins mine and lightens up more of the pit. Still not enough to see clearly, but we can see more of it.

"Is there anyone down there?" I scream into the pit. When there is no reply, I feel tears fill my eyes.

"Maybe they have gagged them," Shok states, now back to his normal self. "Someone needs to go down there to check."

"I'll go, but we need rope," Drez states.

"Who needs rope when I'm around?" Hope mutters as she looks up at Drez. "I will get roots up and around you that will hold you firm."

"Just make sure they don't drop him on his head," Trek mutters as he looks at Hope innocently, and I know that he is trying to get her mind off of what Drez might find down in the pit.

"Well, maybe I will get some roots to hold him and weeds to cover your mouth," she says, which has him grinning at her. She places her hands flat on the ground next to the opening to the pit and closes her eyes. She frowns as she fights her exhaustion to manifest enough energy to bring the right roots to her. It takes her a couple minutes, but finally, there is a root breaking through the ground next to my leg. Its progress isn't as rapid as I know it can be, but at least she is managing to get it up and through the opening down into the darkness.

"I think that is enough," Trek says as he comes to stand behind her, placing his hands on her shoulders. I see him squeeze gently in comfort.

“The trick is going to be for you to fit in this opening,” I state as I look up at Drez and then at the opening with the covering still half obscuring the space.

“Don’t worry, it’s just a tight fit trying to get through the opening. Once I’m in, it’s more spacious,” he says as he picks up the root.

“How do you know that?” I ask with a frown.

“Because I have been down there before. All of us have. It is part of our training; we stay down there for two days before climbing back out.”

I gasp at the thought. “That’s terrible,” I say, sure that I am looking appalled.

“No, it just hardens us for this type of eventuality.” With that, he smiles at me before he places his feet on the brim of the hole and starts to use the root to climb down. He squeezes into the pit until I can only see his head, and then lowers himself. My heart is racing, not only because I’m worried about what might be at the bottom, but I’m worried about Drez. He might be the Demon slayer, but he is still just an Elf who can be killed.

I look into the pit until I can’t see him any longer. “It’s so dark down there,” I comment.

"Yes, it is. Imagine being down there for days," Love says in a strained voice. I can hear the worry in her tone.

"How are you doing down there?" Trek calls.

"Nearly there," Drez replies. We all wait anxiously, awaiting to know what he will find. "They are here."

Tears fill my eyes as I await to know if they are okay. It takes what seems like hours for him to give us an update, but it can't be more than a few minutes. "Pull our sovereign up." Immediately, Shok is pulling it up slowly.

And then I see what looks like the top of my mom's head. Trek is there leaning into the pit and pulling her up. The tears I was holding at bay fall unchecked as I see the dishevelled Fairy being pulled out. Her clothes are tattered and torn, her hair matted with mud, but the most important part is that she has her eyes open and is squinting at the brightness of being in daylight again.

"Mom," Love whispers as she strokes her cheek, pulling the gag off. She tries to speak, but her voice is crackly and she immediately starts to cough. Trek hurries to the haversack that we usually carry our things in and pulls out a skin of water that we carry with us. Bringing it to Love, he stands back, seeing her wetting my mom's lips.

I hear Shok telling Drez that he is sending down the root. My mom tries again, and this time, her words are understandable. "Dad . . ."

"Yes, Mom, they're bringing him up," Hope says as she strokes her fingers.

"He . . . needs . . ." Her voice breaks again as she takes a deep breath, her eyes watering badly from the light.

"Love, move over so you cover the light," I murmur.

"Needs your . . . help," she finishes.

"Our king is coming up," I hear Drez call, and then Shok and Trek pull him up. When he reaches the top, both men bend down, pulling him through the hole into the light. Immediately, I can tell that his wounds are draining his life force. Now that I see what looks like various cuts and a gaping wound on his leg, I understand my mother's anxiety to have us help him.

"Dad?" I call, but contrary to my mother, he doesn't open his eyes or show any sign of being conscious. "We need to clean his wounds." Hope, too, comes to see the damage.

"Use your . . . gifts," Mom murmurs as she slowly stretches out her hand to touch my dad's leg.

"Oh, Mom, we can't. We all depleted our energy trying to bring down the magic that was holding you," Love states as she lowers her head and kisses her forehead. She then helps her drink a little more water.

"Why don't you . . ."—she takes a deep breath before continuing—"energize?"

I continue looking at all the wounds on Dad's body.

"How do we do that?" Hope asks as she glances over her shoulder at Mom.

"Your powers use the source." Her voice is becoming stronger.

"What do you mean?" I ask. Is there some kind of talisman that we need to have that helps us not deplete our energy?

"Hope . . . from the earth." I can see the effort of talking is tiring her. "Dream, the sun." She raises her hand to stroke Love's cheek. "And, you, from . . . love around you."

I frown at her explanation; how do I energize from the sun?

"But how, Mom?" Hope asks as she takes the skin from Love and starts to wet Dad's lips.

"Pull to you," she murmurs as she closes her eyes. I raise my brows at Hope as we look at each other.

"I think what she means is that we pull the energy to us like we have been doing with each other's."

"But I can't touch the sun," I mutter as I see Drez being helped out of the pit.

"As you manifest it, I'm guessing just bring it to you," Love says with a frown.

"I'll try," Hope says. Closing her eyes, she places her hands flat on the ground. After a minute or two, I see small flowers start to spring around her hands, but besides that, I can't tell if it's working. I pick up the skin of water from the ground that Hope has placed there and start to clean the smaller wounds.

After a few minutes, Hope opens her eyes, and I notice they are a vivid green, a radiant smile across her face. "That is amazing. Why didn't I know about this before?" Well, I guess it works. "You need to try it. I will start helping Dad, and you join me when you're done."

"Okay, let me try." Standing, I walk to where a ray of sun is shining down on the ground, lighting that area. Standing right below it, I close my eyes and lift my head to the sun. Feeling its warm substance warm me, I feel the particles enter through every pore in my body, flowing through my veins and energizing me. I don't know how long I stay like this, but it feels amazing, peaceful, and like I am bigger than life. Opening my eyes, I look around, seeing everything with a radiance I haven't seen before. Wow, it is amazing.

Turning, I see that Drez is standing just a few feet away, keeping an eye on me. Smiling at him, I nod. "It works." He smiles and then nods.

"Come, let's go help the king." He holds out his hand, which surprises me, but I take the offered hand, making our way towards the others. Kneeling next to Dad, I place my hands on him and send light shining through his body, clearing away any infection that might have started to set in. When I feel that I have done what I can, I sit back.

"Love, shall we swap?" It's her turn to come and give my dad comfort while I do what I can for Mom. Just as I'm about to stand, Dad opens his eyes.

"Dream," he whispers.

"Dad, you're going to be okay," I murmur as I smile at him.

"Drez?"

Why is he asking for Drez?

"I am here, my king," Drez replies, kneeling so that he can see him.

"There is a traitor. Trust no one here." He closes his eyes, his breathing laboured, but then he opens them again, looking directly at Drez. "Tell her." And with that, he falls into unconsciousness again.

"What did he mean?" I ask, frowning. Taking my hand as he stands and helps me up, Drez guides me a few steps away from the others and then faces me. I stand before him, looking up into his handsome face as strokes his fingers through his hair—a sign of nervousness, something I have noticed before but that he doesn't do often.

"There is a reason I was sent to Eternity Fae," he starts by saying, and I realize that he hasn't let go of my hand, which has warmth radiating from him up my arm and through my body.

"Yes, as one of our guards," I say, inclining my head.

"No," he says as he shakes his head. "As your protector."

I tense. What does that mean?

"The first time I went with our sovereigns to Eternity Fae and met you, I knew."

"What?" He is making no sense.

"That you are mine." I feel my heart lurch. "You are my mate, Dream."

What? My mind goes blank.

"I told the sovereigns when we got back here that you are my mate, and they assigned me to you, asking me to only tell you when it was time."

"We're mates?" I ask, and he smiles at my bemused expression.

"Yes, we are." He lifts his hand to the side of my face, stroking it gently. "And I have wanted to do this for the longest time." I see his head lowering to mine. Even if I wanted to run, my legs wouldn't cooperate. When his lips touch mine for the first time, it's like an explosion of feelings, of memories rushing through my mind, my body. All this time, I loved Drez and he loved me back. I know that our journey is just beginning and these are turbulent times, but with him at my side, we can conquer any evil that comes our way.

TO BE CONTINUED WITH THE RISE OF THE WARLOCK (BOOK 2)

A MESSAGE FROM ALEXI FERREIRA

Thank you so much for reading THE FORCE OF FIVE book. This is the first book of the Eternity Fae series. I hope you enjoyed your journey into the life of these strong fairy sisters. **If you enjoyed this book, please consider leaving a review. Reviews help authors like me stay visible and help bring others to my series**. Next book in the series will be HOPE, but it will also allow you to carry on following Dream's adventure.

THE RISE OF THE WARLOCK

CHAPTER 1

It has been a month since we were able to vanquish the noise from the property and get rid of all the shadows and caped shadows in the city but we still can't get into Eternity Fae Forest, the forest is still protected against anyone going in or out. Dream has been painting her room as it is at Eternity Fae so that she can go there through the painting and let the others know what is happening.

Drez was opposed to the idea at first but when Dream suggested that he go with her he came around. Ever since the moment that Drez opened up to Dream to tell her that they are in fact mates that they have been inseparable. I am happy for the two of them, they make such a cute couple and we all knew how Dream felt about Drez ever since she met him, but he was a dark horse and was able to hide his feelings well.

We have let everyone back to their posts once we got everything up and running again but we know that there is someone in the kitchen that is responsible for what happened here before.

Someone poisoned the food previously so that when the shadows attacked the guards were mostly debilitated. The Gargoyles on the turrets are still grotesques and no matter what we have tried we haven't been able to turn them back into themselves. One of those Gargoyles is Shok's brother which has him up in arms turning every rock trying to find who is responsible for this.

Yesterday Trek, Shok my mom the Sovereign Fairy Queen and two of the guards went once again to the border of Eternity Fae to see if they could somehow find a way in. My Dad is still not up to going anywhere as the magic that was used on him has taken longer to heal than others that have been attacked before. Dream, Love and myself have been healing his wounds every couple of days, extracting the darkness from his wounds and filling him with Love and Hope but we need Reality and Vain here to add their magic to his healing as he gets better and then after a couple of days the infections starts setting in again.

"Hope!" I look over my shoulder at Dream to see her looking at me with a frown, "You didn't hear a thing I said did you?"

"Sorry I was looking at the guards training outside" my mind was actually far from the training and the guards there, but I don't tell Dream that. I turn to look at Dream to find that the drawing that she has done on the wall is now finished, it looks just like her room at Eternity Fae. "You finished" I state as I take a step closer.

"Yes, that's what I was saying" I look at her to see her still frowning. "Hope I'm not sure if this will work, before I was only able to see what I painted, I'm not sure that there is anything else outside of the painting."

"You worry to much Dream, it will be fine just don't forget to think of a way to get back when you going in or you will be stuck at Eternity Fae without us, and to be honest I would rather you be here."

"Aww Hope, are you saying that you would miss me?" Dream teases, "I thought that your arguments with Trek kept you entertained enough." I pull my tongue out at her in reply, it is true that most of the time we pick on each other more as entertainment then arguing but Trek can also be stubborn and drives me crazy most of the time as he tries to order me around.

I know that he's my personal guard and as such he needs to make sure that I am safe, but he doesn't have to be so condescending.

"Are you missing him Hope?" Love asks from where she's sitting on the floor reading a romance book. Love is a hopeless romance and as her name predicts sees love everywhere.

"No, why would I be missing him" I ask sarcastically, "he irritates me most of the time,"

"well I think you missing him" Love says with a cheeky grin and a wink at Dream

"Stop doing that, I just think that mom should have let me go with them, I might have been able to help. I'm not missing him." In truth I am missing him but maybe just a little.

"She's very defensive isn't she Love?" Dream asks playfully

"Don't you start too" I mutter looking at Dream that simply grins at me, "anyway to more important things," I say trying to get their minds away from me. "I was thinking that we should monitor more carefully what Dad is eating. I find it very strange how the darkness keeps on coming back only after a couple of day and its never the same amount of days, sometimes its longer and sometimes shorter periods."

“You think someone is doing something to keep him like that?” Love asks as she stands, closing her book and placing it on the bed besides her.

“I’m not sure, it just seems strange.” I state

“I agree with you, I have been thinking it strange too.” Dream states, “I mean when we heal him there is no darkness left, how does it come back?”

“Maybe lets go and see if there is anything that he uses that might be manifesting this onto him or we will have to take turns and stay with him, see everything that he drinks, eats or touches that might be doing this.” I say as I look at both my sisters

“You know what I have been thinking,” Dream says as she starts packing her paints and brushes. “Maybe I could start by going into each person’s dreams at night and try and find out if any one of them is the traitor.”

“Do you think you could pick it up from their dreams?” I ask

“I’m not sure, but I’m sure I might see darkness in them and would know” Dream replies as she turns towards us, cleaning her hands on a rag. “I’m ready shall we go see Dad” she says

The three of us make our way out of the room and down the corridor towards our parents room, "You could try, I have been looking at peoples energy, some are darker than others but nothing that would call out traitor." Love says, Love has always been able to see people's aura, or the colour of their energy and usually know if they were good or bad. For her not to have seen anyone standing out I wonder if the person is even someone that works in the property or if maybe just someone that comes to deliver things.

"You can do that with things too can't you Love?" I ask as an idea starts materializing

"Yes of course, I have learned with time to block it and only see it when I want to but I can see the energy of people, animals, vegetation and even things when someone has touched it." I see her eyes widening as she says the last. "Of course," she says with a smile and a wink at me. "I can see if there is anything in Dad's room with a bad energy and that might lead us to who has put it there."

We enter our parents room to see Dad sitting up in bed glaring at Thomas my parents right hand and advisor. When he sees us his expression changes and he opens his arms for us to go to him. His wings are peeking out from behind him which tells me that he has been up and stretching them out sometime earlier.

"What's wrong Daddy," Love says as she sits on his right hugging him across his stomach and kissing his cheek. His arm wraps around her and he lowers his head to kiss her head. Dream and I are standing at the bottom of the bed as Thomas is still standing next to the bed on my Dad's left-hand side.

"Nothing my angel, its all good." His voice is gravely and low, "You can go Thomas" he mutters, and I see Thomas tenses, but he nods, turns and then leaves. Dream moves towards where Thomas was and sits down on Dad's left-hand side, his arm stretches out and he takes her hand in his smiling at her. "Why are you so far Hope, come closer." I climb onto the bed, crawling up I sit just behind Dream, her back to my front.

"So, are you going to tell us why you are so upset but are trying to hide it?" I ask with a raised brow which has him looking at me and then shaking his head as he grins.

"You are just like your mother, doesn't mince her words." He says, and then shrugs, "I'm just tired of being in bed and I should be by your mothers' side, what if there is an attack?" his frown is back

"You know that mom can take care of herself, and she has four guards with her." Dream says as she strokes his fingers, "besides mom said that you would stay here to protect us." I see Dad raise a brow and look at her.

"Are you trying to appease me Dream?" and then he shakes his head, "I have missed this, I wish Reality and Vain were also here."

"Don't worry about that, Dream has finished her painting, tonight she will go and let the others know that we are fine and what they need to look out for." Love says with a smile, her head against his chest.

"Are you sure this will work? I don't want you to get stuck in a painting and then we can't get you out of there." He states as he lifts his hand to stroke Dream's cheek.

"Yes Dad, I have done it before." Dream says with a smile

"I don't like you girls experimenting with your magic when there is no supervision, Selina was there to guide you, to teach you." He mutters

"We are fine," I say which has him grunting, "more importantly, how are you feeling today?"

“You healed me yesterday, so I’m good.” He says with a shrug

“Well we have had an idea.” I say, and go on to explain what we are thinking of doing to find if in fact someone is still manifesting evil somehow in the property or if its some kind of magic that was used when they wounded my dad.

“I swear if we find a traitor in this house they will pay” he grunts angrily

“Well, I shall start” Love says as she sits up and then starts to look around the room, suddenly she frowns and then is crawling out of bed and towards my Dad’s side table where a pitcher with water is sitting and a glass. Next to it is a plate that is covered with a napkin and which seems like Dad has not eaten yet.

“Whatever is on this plate hasn’t got good energy” Love mutters, Dad leans over and pulls the napkin away to show us a plate with two scones on it.

“You saying the scone is doing this to me?” he asks with a frown; I stand to go and smell the scone. If there is any poisonous ingredient, I will be able to detect it. Leaning down I take a whiff of the scone, but I can’t detect anything, unless this is magic.

"There is nothing to indicate it's an herb or poison." I say

"I don't think It's the scone, I see the energy on the pitcher of water and glass too." Love says, "I think its whoever touched these items that has left this trail of energy, but this might not be what is doing this to Dad."

"Well I think I'm going to go into the kitchen and see what is happening there, maybe I might find something." I state as I turn

"I will go with you, Love maybe you should stay here and keep Dad company." Dream says

"Definitely, and I still want to look at all the other things in the room and anyone that might come in."

"You girls be careful, where is Drez? He should be going with you if Shok and Trek arent' here." Dad says as we stop in the doorway.

"He was traying with the guards, I'm sure he will be up soon." Dream says, "Don't worry we can take care of ourselves." As we walk out of the room, we here Dad grunt at Dreams reply which has me smiling.

"He still thinks of us as his little girls." I state as we hurry downstairs

"I think he will always think of us like that." Dream says as we walk, glancing at Dream I realize that once again she has left her bow somewhere.

"Where did you leave your bow?" at my question her hand snaps up towards her shoulder and she frowns.

"Argh, I left it in my room" she is becoming better, but she still forgets her bow a lot and at these times we need to make sure that we are always protected. My weapon of choice is my fighting sticks, I was lucky to have got these retractable ones for my birthday from Trek, they fit on a holster to my waste. "It just becomes so cumbersome when I'm doing something." She mutters

"Maybe you should think of using some other type of weapon." I say, knowing that she will reject the idea. All of us have been trained with different weapons, but we have all excelled in one and that one is usually the one that we have chosen to mainly fight with. Dream is the bow, she can shoot anything out of the air while in flight, she is an exceptional marksman but that's when she is actually using the bow.

With me it has always been the sticks, at first it was only one but with time I have enhanced my movements and rhythm and now am able to use a fighting stick in each hand with the same speed and accuracy as I was doing with just one. I also train daily to maintain my movements supple and fluid.

Arriving in the kitchen I see the chef standing over one of the cooks commenting on what he is doing. There are two others that are sorting out vegetables, one cutting meat two in the dishes area and then I see two of the serving ladies and one guard are also here.

When we walk in everyone stops what they are doing and looks at us, then the Chef is walking towards us a smile on his face. “Do you need anything?” he asks

“No, just continue with your work we are just here to observe” I say which has the Chef’s smile turning into a frown.

“Is there a problem?” he asks quietly

“No, no problem” Dream says with a gentle smile, I see the guard and the serving ladies leaving.

“Chef, do staff usually come into the kitchen to eat or is there a specific area for them?” I don’t see a table here like there is at Eternity Fae so there must be an area where they all eat. He turns slightly to show us a door to our left.

"Through there is where everyone comes to eat, we always have someone there to serve them." He says, "and through there is where we serve our Sovereigns, the guard and of course you."

"Are you the only chef in the kitchen at all times?" I know he won't be, but I thought I would ask, he shakes his head.

"No, there is one more, but he will be in later."

"Is there any reason at all for any other staff to be in the kitchen besides the kitchen staff?" he scratches his jaw, a frown marring his forehead but then he shakes his head.

"No,"

"Good, from now on please make sure that only kitchen staff enter here." I state, "If you don't mind we are just going to hang around for a little bit, please don't let us disturb you." I can see that he wants to ask us why but he must realize that we wont be saying anything so he nods and leaves. Dream walks towards a chair on one of the sides and takes a seat. I know that she will be trying to see the darkness from where she is in each person, I move towards where the food is being prepared.

It is time to see if there is any poison in this kitchen or anything that might be turned into poison.

Printed in Great Britain
by Amazon

26249256R00128